About the author

Born in 1968, TS O'Rourke grew up in Tipperary, Cork and Dublin. He has lived in Australia, the UK and Sweden. He works as an editor and advertising copywriter. His first novel, Ganglands, was published in 1996, followed a year later by Death Call.

Also by the same author

Ganglands
Death Call

Dedication:

For
James O'Rourke
Dublin Brigade IRA
Executed in Beggar's Bush Barracks
March 1923

Acknowledgements

The author would like to thank the following
individuals for their continued encouragement:
Carina, Molly, Jamey, Jason O'Toole,
Gavin Murphy, Sam & Mary O'Rourke,
and Donal & Miriam O'Donovan.

THE
REPUBLICAN

TS O'ROURKE

Killynon
HouseBooks

Chapter One

Dublin, March 1922

The fresh leaves of spring were breaking through on the young trees that lined Usher's Quay. Jack and Kathy walked slowly towards the Four Courts on the banks of the River Liffey. It was Jack's first full day off duty in over a month.

Crossing Whitworth Bridge they moved up past the courts, grateful that they had a little time alone together. The past few months had been hard. Since the Treaty had been signed there had been much confusion and division in the country, with both the newly formed Free State Army and the Republican Army vying for position.

Jack and his comrades were on full alert, carrying out occasional raids on government offices and banks in an effort to disrupt the workings of the acting government and raise the money necessary to support their number. The government had supported them until quite recently. Things had changed quickly. The government was now intent on forcing through measures that would put a squeeze on those opposing the Treaty. Everyone was waiting for this uneasy peace to come to an abrupt end, as the opposing parties clashed in the Dáil.

Kathy turned to Jack, looked up into his blue eyes and smiled.

'I hope it doesn't get any worse. I hate thinking how dangerous it is when you're out with the unit.'

'I'm in no danger, darling. Sure don't I have the lads of the Dublin Brigade behind me?' Jack said in an effort to dismiss Kathy's fears.

'You know what I mean. Poor Mrs. Kearney lost her son James last year in that attack on Portobello Barracks, and she hasn't been the same since. And now her other son has joined up.'

'Well we'll have to see what de Valera has to say on the matter—he seems to have changed his mind since the Treaty was signed and the lads in the Dublin Brigade, well, most of them won't accept the terms of the Treaty either. We're with O'Connor and Mellows.'

'I hope this is an end to the fighting, once and for all,' Kathy said, staring out across the Liffey.

The smoke from a Guinness boat could be seen rising beyond Butt Bridge as it made its way out into the Irish Sea, laden with barrels of the black stuff. Seagulls swooped and cried as they moved ever inland, predicting bad weather in the coming days, while Dublin struggled towards normality after months of war. The bells of St. Michan's pealed reassuringly as lines of well-dressed office workers filed down along the quays on their way home from work, while barefoot children from the nearby tenements attempted to skim stones over the surface of the river.

'Don't you think it strange the way de Valera changed his mind once the Treaty had been rejected by the Republican Army?' Kathy asked, her mind once again returning to the present political situation.

'Not really—Dev is a political animal—he knows that he stands a better chance on the side of the Republicans than he does with the government—sure him and Collins are always at each others' throats,' Jack said, staring over towards Christ Church Cathedral.

'But it won't come to war, will it?' Kathy wondered, afraid that her worst fears might be soon realised.

'I don't know,' Jack replied, looking out across the river.

All that Kathy had wanted since the Black and Tan War ended was to ensure that Jack came to no harm, so that they could be married next year. She had envisioned a glorious spring day in their parish church, off Gardiner Street. The local priest, Father Murphy, had presided over her sister's wedding the year before and it had been a lovely ceremony.

As they passed the Ha'penny Bridge they could see a crowd gathering up by O'Connell Bridge, with much confusion and anticipation in the air. Over one hundred people had gathered on the bridge. They appeared to be waiting for something to happen. One or two men, whom Jack immediately recognised as Free State Army recruiting officers, tried to hold the crowd back from what appeared to be a platform of some description. He had fought with both of the men during the Black and Tan War, but they were now on the other side, spreading lies about their former comrades and selling out the ideal of a Republic. Jack could feel his hackles rise at the mere sight of the Free Staters' uniforms.

'I wonder what's happening,' Kathy said, as Jack's eyes scanned the crowd ahead of him. Their job, Jack thought, was to prevent any interference in the proceedings by Republican sympathisers.

Jack and Kathy's pace increased as they saw a man climb up on a platform with his back to them. He began to speak. As he did so a broad young man in a beige raincoat began shouting insults at the speaker. He was quickly ejected from the circle of listeners. The man made his way toward

Jack and Kathy, a smile on his face.

'Jack!' the man called. 'Jack! They're holding a convention tonight.'

The man was Jimmy O'Toole, a member of Jack's battalion in the Dublin Brigade. He had been a close friend of Jack's for years.

'What's that?' Jack asked, struggling to hear his friend over the speaker on the bridge.

'There's to be a convention tonight. Lynch, Brugha, O'Connor and the rest of them are going to speak—it looks like we might be finally making a move. There's been talk of it for weeks,' Jimmy said.

'Talk of what?' Kathy asked.

'Talk of asserting the Republic,' Jack said, knowing that it would upset her.

'What do you mean asserting the Republic?' Kathy questioned.

'He means fighting for it. There's almost a fifty-fifty split between those in favour of the Free State and those for continuing the struggle for the Republic,' Jimmy said.

'So when did they decide to hold a convention?' Jack asked, feeling Kathy's hand under his jacket on the small of his back.

'We were told last night over at the HQ. I was told to spread the word to the volunteers from our battalion who weren't there last night. It's being held tonight at eight o'clock,' Jimmy said.

'Where?'

'Over in City Hall. It looks like they might be putting the question to us.'

'What question?' Kathy asked, in an effort to understand the half-code that the two volunteers used without thinking.

'Whether we are prepared to continue the fight,' Jack

said, holding Kathy close to him.

'I'd better be off—I've got to visit a few of the lads and spread the word. I'll see you later,' Jimmy said, nodding politely to Kathy before dashing off in the direction of Dame Street.

Kathy's mind flashed back to how things had been before the Treaty had been signed. She had hardly seen Jack from one end of the month to the other—and even then only fleetingly. The constant fear of British Army reprisals and raids on Republican households before the truce had kept most activists on the run. Most volunteers had relied on the many safe houses in the city for food and lodging between surprise attacks on columns of Black and Tans and regular British army troops as they patrolled the streets. But that was all over for the moment. Now, the thought of Irishmen fighting Irishmen filled her head. Surely there could be nothing worse than that, she thought, clutching Jack's arm tightly.

'We'd best start making our way home,' Jack said, thinking that it was time to take Kathy back to her mother's house.

Kathy lived just five doors up from where Jack had been born and reared. Their families were close and they had been friends all of their lives. It was a small, close-knit community where everyone knew everyone else's business and where neighbours helped each other when times were hard. And times had indeed been hard in recent years. Half of the street's men had either been killed in the Great War or had spent a year or two in prison after the 1916 Rising, leaving many families without an income. It was the sense of quiet desperation that had formed a unique bond in their street and in many other streets around the city.

Jack's mind began to spin at the thought of the army convention. How would he vote? Did he really want to go back to war? These questions bedevilled him as he walked Kathy home. He knew that Rory O'Connor and Liam Mellows wanted to oppose the acting government and continue to disrupt it as much as possible, but how far they were intent on going he did not know. Since the Dáil vote in January there had been something of a stand-off between those in favour of and those opposing the Treaty, but Jack had never thought the issue would lead them to the brink of civil war. Both pro- and anti-Treaty units had been patrolling the city and it had been getting very tense of late. It was only a matter of time before shots would be fired in anger.

It seemed incredible that Irishmen could take up arms against their former comrades, who were, after all, only continuing the fight that they had all pledged to see to the bitter end. It was a matter of loyalty, courage and conviction. No amount of propaganda from either side could make Jack see things differently. It was clear-cut and obvious in his mind.

As de Valera had recently said in a speech in Dungarvan, and which he later defended in the press, 'if you don't fight today, you'll have to fight tomorrow; and I say, when you are in a good fighting position, then fight on.' These words had rattled through the brains of every Irishman in the land that had at one time picked up a rifle to achieve Irish freedom and create a Republic. And it was these words, along with the many late-night discussions that Jack had had with his commanding officers and fellow volunteers that had hardened his resolve. If a Republic was within sight, then it should be fought for—whatever the outcome. He knew that he would vote for action, whatever happened.

The spring day was beginning to darken as Kathy and

Jack made their way up Gardiner Street towards Gloucester Place.

'When do you have some more time off?' Kathy asked, wondering when she would see him again.

'I don't know, darling, it'll all depend on what happens tonight.'

'Don't go voting for trouble, will you?' Kathy pleaded. She knew what he had in mind.

'I'll listen to what the lads have to say tonight and then I'll make my decision. I want to avoid war as much as anyone else does, but we've come so far in the last few years. It would be a sin to give it all away when we are so close to getting what we want,' Jack said, his line of vision now filled with the sight of children playing football on their street.

'Just remember that the most important thing in the world is you and me. Then everything will work out fine,' Kathy said, hoping that Jack's sense of loyalty and commitment could be re-directed to where it mattered most.

'Don't worry,' Jack replied, 'I'm doing all of this for you and the family. Someone has to do it. I know what I'm doing,' he continued, as if to justify his intentions.

Jack's thoughts turned on seeing his family home.

'Do you want to come in for a cup of tea?' he asked. 'I'm sure my Ma would be happy to see you.'

'No, I'd best be getting home. I've got to help my mother make dinner—my father will be home from work soon,' Kathy replied, giving Jack a quick kiss on the cheek, before running up the road. She turned as she reached the front door of the house and smiled.

She is truly beautiful, Jack thought, seeing her long black hair and the glint of affection in her dark brown eyes. There never could be another.

Jack entered his mother's house to find his cousin Terry

seated at the kitchen table. He was also in the Dublin Brigade, attached to a south side unit operating out of the Cuffe Street area, just off St. Stephen's Green. He had seen his fair share of action over the last two years and had been badly wounded in an attack on a column of Black and Tans on Wexford Street. He was still limping from his wound but was back on active service. Terry could never sit still while a fight was going on, Jack thought to himself with a smile.

Once Jack announced his news of the convention, the Larkin household went strangely quiet. Jack's sister, Helen, was busying herself around the house, while his mother sat quietly contemplating the possible outcome of an army convention. She knew that it could mean only one thing: war.

It had been the same in Easter 1916 when Jack's father had attended his weekly Irish Volunteer meetings and a general call to arms had been made. But on that occasion countermanding orders had also been issued, resulting in a poor turn out for the Rising, which doomed it to failure from the outset and ultimately led to the death of her husband.

She had seen the Irish Volunteers, her husband amongst them, proudly marching, meeting, and planning to fight for a Republic. It seemed like only yesterday that she was seeing her man walk out the door, his Mauser rifle newly oiled and gleaming in the spring sunshine as he marched off to fight and die. And now her son was following in his footsteps. Will there be no end to it, she thought, seeing the excitement in the eyes of the two young men as Helen got caught up in the moment.

Helen's boyfriend, Barry Murphy, another of Jack's comrades, was sure to be there and Helen wanted to hear what the boys were thinking. She dished out a plate of cabbage and potatoes covered with some dripping from that morning's breakfast of rashers and pudding. Jack sat down at the kitchen table. Terry smiled hungrily as Jack began to eat. It looked like it could be a long night, what with the convention and all of the talking that was ahead of them. And after that, well, they were sure to repair to a local public house to cool their throats from the talking. It was as wise to fill up now, Terry thought, savouring the first mouthful.

'Could I come along tonight?' Helen asked, wiping her hands on her skirt.

'Sorry, Helen,' Jack said, 'but it's only volunteers that are allowed to attend. I'll tell you all about it later tonight when I get back.'

'Tell Barry to call around if you see him, will you? I haven't heard from him in over a week,' Helen said, wondering what he had been up to.

'I'll bring him back with me tonight if he can come,' Jack said.

'You'll do no such thing and the neighbours twitching their curtains,' Jack's mother said, thinking of the noise that drunken and war-hungry men would make after a bellyful of beer.

'Well, ask him to call around tomorrow,' Helen said, slightly disappointed at her mother's reaction.

'We'll probably run into him,' Jack said. 'He's always near the front at these meetings.'

'Do you fancy having a half-one before we go in?' Terry asked, devouring another mouthful of cabbage and potatoes.

'We could go over to Mulligan's for a quick one, I suppose. There's bound to be a few of the lads around,' Jack replied.

He had been frequenting Mulligan's Public House since

the age of sixteen, when he had earned his first wage as a delivery boy for a local butcher. But once the War of Independence had begun in earnest, there had been little time for socialising and drinking.

'It's far from public houses you two ought to be keeping with all the commotion that has been going on,' Jack's mother said sharply, poking the fire to life and adding a few pieces of turf to the burning embers.

'A small one won't do us any harm,' Terry said with a smile. 'Sure it'll just put us in a mood for the meeting.'

'Well take care that it's you and not the whiskey that's doing the voting later on!' the old woman warned, smoothing down her skirts and sitting back in her chair.

'Don't worry, Ma, I'll look after him!' Jack said with a smile, lightening the tension.

'It's somebody to look after the two of you that you need. It's the blind leading the blind!' she replied, smiling at her only son, before looking up at the picture of her dead husband.

Silence descended on the room. Terry and Jack continued to eat until they had cleared their plates. Helen brought them both a mug of sweet tea and a piece of fruitcake.

'You're too good to us, Helen,' Terry said.

'Ah you need it—sure you're nothing but a bag of bones! When was the last time you had a decent meal?' Jack's mother asked.

'Oh, it must be about a week ago—the last time I went to see my sister and her family,' Terry said.

Terry's parents and younger brother had died in a fire less than two years ago. The blaze was started when the Black and Tans raided some rooms in the tenement where they lived. Terry's parents had lived on the top floor and by the time they were aware of the fire it was too late.

Since that time Terry had taken part in every attack on the Tans that had been carried out on the south side of the city, ambushing them in the narrow city centre streets, and throwing paraffin and petrol bombs into their open-topped Crossley tenders.

In an effort to stop the Republicans from throwing fire-bombs into the personnel carriers the British Army had built small wooden frames covered in chicken wire that they placed over the backs of their vehicles. At first their attackers didn't quite know what to do, but soon came up with firebombs that bore little hooks, so they would attach themselves to the wire. As a result, the chicken-coops, as the tenders became known, were not the favourite form of transport of the occupying army.

Jack stood up from the table, grabbed his jacket and hat and waited by the door.

'Come on Terry, get a move on. It's nearly seven o'clock!' he said, hoping his cousin would rise from the table, where he sat back, rubbing his belly.

'I'll be right with you,' Terry said, making a move to get up.

'Be careful out there. The Civic Guards are just looking for an excuse to lock Republicans up these days—so don't go causing any trouble,' Mrs. Larkin warned as she helped Helen clear the dinner table.

'Don't worry, Ma, I'll keep my head down and I'll see to it that Terry does too,' Jack replied, patting Terry on the back in an effort to hurry him along. He knew it would take a good fifteen minutes to get to Mulligan's Public House with Terry limping like he did and he wanted to be where the action and discussion was as soon as was humanly possible.

Terry put his jacket on and reached for his flat cap and overcoat before turning to the two women who were starting to do the washing-up.

'Thanks again for the dinner, Auntie Mary, and you too, Helen,' Terry said appreciatively.

'No bother,' Mrs. Larkin replied. 'I'm always happy to see you, Terry. Don't leave it so long before you visit us next time and take good care of yourself now, do you hear?'

'I will. C'mon, lets go,' Terry said to Jack, who shook his head in disbelief.

The two men made their way out into the cool night air and began their walk down Gardiner Street towards the Customs House. Having crossed Butt Bridge they soon found sanctuary in Mulligan's of Poolbeg Street.

The sound of clinking glasses and raised voices greeted the two men as they entered the public house and made their way through the crowd to the bar. There, standing with his back to them, was none other than Cathal Brugha—one of the leading Republicans in Dublin, if not the country.

Brugha was a small man and a ferocious fighter. He had gained a reputation as both a military strategist and a clever politician over the last number of years. He had been negotiating with de Valera in recent weeks and it looked like he was bringing de Valera around to his way of thinking.

Jack nudged Terry in the ribs as he lifted two creamy pints of porter from the old wooden counter.

'There's Brugha,' Jack said nodding towards the man with obvious admiration.

'Are you sure?' Terry asked.

'I'd recognise him anywhere. He was with us on an attack against the Tans last year and he made sure we got the better of them.'

Terry looked around to see whom else he might recognise.

'And he's talking to Liam Lynch,' Terry said.

Lynch was an IRA man from the south, who commanded most of the southern counties. His men were fiercely loyal to him.

'It looks like they're all here tonight,' Jack said, before taking a mouthful of stout.

'Something big is happening, I can feel it,' Terry replied.

'Lynch would have hardly come all the way up from Cork for this meeting if there wasn't something big in the air,' Jack remarked.

'You can bet your life on it.'

Cathal Brugha turned around and addressed Jack.

'Don't I know you from somewhere?'

'Yes sir, I'm Jack Larkin. I was with you in an attack against the Tans last year off Thomas Street.'

'I thought I recognised your face. Are you going over to the meeting?' Brugha asked, by way of finding out if they were anti-Treaty volunteers.

'Yes, sir, that we are. I was just saying to Terry here that it looks like something big is going to happen tonight. Has a decision been made about the government?' Jack asked, lowering his voice.

Brugha took a step closer to Jack and replied in a whisper, changing from English to Irish as he spoke. Most volunteers had learned to speak a little Irish over the last number of years—many of them in British prisons after 1916. Jack had learned the language while he was a member of Fianna na hÉireann, the Republican movement's answer to Baden-Powell's boy scout organisation. Apart from the military training Fianna members did, they had spent a good deal of time studying history and the Irish language.

'There's been a lot of talking over the last few weeks and a few decisions have been made—but decisions are no good without the backing of you lads and the other volunteers. That's why we've called this meeting,' Brugha replied.

'Is it back to war with Britain we're going, Mr. Brugha?' Terry asked.

'That's up to Collins to decide. He's either with us or against us, but he doesn't seem to have made up his mind which way he'll go.'

'Well, we're ready to go back to war,' Jack interjected, 'though it's the last thing we want if it's our own comrades we'll be facing.'

'I hope it doesn't have to come to that. It all depends on Mick Collins and his boys. They've had a bite of Lloyd George's cake and they seem to like it,' Brugha replied.

'Power is a terrible thing to have over so many peoples' lives,' Jack said.

'That's why we need to fight for what we believe in and not just accept what's been given to us. It's all there for the taking, lads. A thirty-two county Republic free from ties with Britain. All it'll take is one more push, and we'll have it.'

Jack nodded in agreement as Brugha smiled and returned to the conversation he was having with Liam Lynch.

'Sounds like we're going back to war,' Jack said, swirling his pint around in his glass.

'It looks like the place is beginning to clear out—we'd best get up to City Hall for this meeting and see what's going to happen,' Terry said, before downing the rest of his drink. It was going to be an interesting night.

Chapter Two

A streaming mass of men in overcoats and caps made their way up Dame Street and filed expectantly into the auditorium of City Hall. Inside at least two hundred and fifty IRA volunteers and battalion commanders talked excitedly of what was to come.

In recent days de Valera had been making speeches around the country, generating much publicity for the anti-Treaty cause.

The acting government didn't like this. In response, Collins and his cohorts had threatened to remove the funding that was keeping many IRA units around the country on their feet. The calling of an army convention, which was going against the grain, was bound to bring down the wrath of Collins and Griffith on the anti-Treaty units.

Questions filled the air. Who would be their new leader if it were decided to act independently of the Dáil? Would a new Republic be proclaimed in the absence of what they believed to be a satisfactory outcome? How would the British react? Would it spark a new war? Which way would Collins go in the face of renewed British aggression that a rejection of the Treaty would inevitably bring about? Only time would tell.

A heady mix of excitement and tension filled the hall as a number of volunteers placed a podium and a few chairs on the stage.

'What do you think Collins will do when he hears about

the convention, Jack?' Thomas Murphy asked. Thomas was a brother to Barry Murphy, who was courting Jack's sister, Helen.

'I'm sure he already knows about it, but he's not going to be a happy man if it goes the way I think it will. I heard yesterday that he's losing control of the south. Cork, Kerry and Tipperary are dead set against the Treaty—most of the units around the country are,' Jack replied.

'Well, this should put an end to the wondering that we've been doing for the last few months. It'll be as well to have it all sorted out once and for all, don't you think?'

'It will. We've been wasting time growing soft, when it's stronger we should be getting. All of this waiting and fundraising isn't solving anything. Better to bring everything to a head and let it sort itself out,' Jack said, Terry nodding with him in agreement.

A voice to their right spoke up in dissension: 'You can't be serious! We've come a long way in the past few months. Sure we were on our knees when the Treaty was signed. If it hadn't been offered the Brits would have beaten us down within a month. I think, despite all of the messing around that Collins and Mulcahy have been doing as regards Ulster, that we should give them a chance to do their best and see what it'll bring. The people don't want another war—they've suffered enough over the last few years to last them a lifetime.'

It was Mick McGinley from the North Circular Road. He and Jack had been in the same unit over the closing months of the Tan War and had agreed on practically everything. Everything, that is, until the Treaty was put before them.

'Jesus, Mick! Will you ever learn? It's the old divide and rule trick that the Brits are pulling on us again. Split us up, create tension, feed disagreements, sit back and watch us tear at each other's throats. Can't you see that?' Terry interjected, as Jack nodded his head in agreement.

'What has all of this been for if not to create a truly independent Republic, free from outside interference? What did our comrades die for over the last few years? Are we going to sell them short because we haven't the guts to fight on for what we believe in?' Jack asked.

'I won't go back to war when there's another route to be taken. We'll still get to the Republic—it'll just take a little longer. But we'll do it politically, peacefully like, you know?' Mick said, hoping to get some degree of agreement.

'You'd sell your own mother to the Brits you cowardly bastard!' Thomas Murphy shouted, attracting the attention of the men in the immediately vicinity.

McGinley took a step forward, grabbed Thomas by the lapels of his coat, and drew his arm back as if to throw a punch. Jack caught his arm and held it, despite McGinley's struggle to connect.

'What did you say?' McGinley asked, daring Thomas to repeat himself.

'You heard what I said you no-good turncoat! Go on with you—fuck off to your British masters and be a good little Irishman for them!' Thomas replied with added venom. 'It's men like you that we need to weed out of the movement.'

A few men in the vicinity began to laugh.

Separating himself from Jack's grip, McGinley took another step back and sneered at Thomas, but the tremble in his hand gave away his fear and uncertainty.

'Give it a rest Mick, for fucksake!' Jack said, hoping to bring a little sense into the situation.

'There'll be time for that after the convention,' Terry agreed.

'You're nothing but a no-good lackey!' McGinley spat, turning and pushing his way through the crowd.

'Jaysus Thomas, you'd start a fight in a confession box!' Jack said with a laugh, trying to calm him down.

'That bastard better not come up against me if it's back to war we're going,' Thomas said.

'There's a load of Civic Guards standing around outside,' Barry Murphy said, unbuttoning his overcoat as he joined the crowd. 'It looks like they're waiting to for us to make up our minds. I wouldn't be surprised if they try to arrest us when we leave,' he said with a grin.

'How have you been?' Jack asked.

'Ah, not too bad. Yourself?'

'We've been trying to keep your brother from getting punched in the head!' Terry said with a laugh.

'What's he on about?' Barry asked Thomas, who did his best to look relaxed.

'Ah, that whore's melt Mick McGinley was spouting off his pro-Treaty line so I told him where to stick it...'

'And McGinley went to give him a punch. You just missed it,' Terry said. 'It was very funny.'

'I'll give the bastard funny. Next time I see him he'd better be ready,' Barry replied. He was always quick to jump to his brother's defence.

'Ah, forget it, Barry, it was Thomas who was causing the problem—McGinley's just an auld eejit. Don't mind him. He's not worth it. His day will come,' Jack said, giving Barry a thump on the shoulder.

'So how's Helen?' Barry asked.

'Jaysus,' Terry said, 'we'll be fighting again in a minute. First it's politics, now it's women, next thing you know it'll be religion!'

'Shut up, Terry!' Jack said playfully. 'She's fine. She was asking for you.'

'Aye, she was. She was wondering why you hadn't been up to visit her. I told her that she should be looking for a better class of volunteer,' Terry finished with a smirk.

Barry grabbed Terry in a headlock and the two men wrestled playfully for a couple of seconds until Jack separated them.

'Stop your messing around, will you, O'Connor's getting up to speak.'

An expectant silence, broken only by the occasional whisper, filled the hall. The cool night air was replaced with a moist mixture of smells. A hundred wet woollen overcoats began to dry slowly in the body heat of the hall. Men shifted anxiously from foot to foot listening intently to Rory O'Connor as he addressed the convention.

O'Connor's commanding voice and presence filled the auditorium as his words made clear the blurred tangle of ideas that lay within the hearts and minds of many volunteers. A man skilled in presenting his case, O'Connor let questions hang in the air, that they might slowly descend, transformed now into answers in the minds of those before him. With his gaunt, chiselled features, and his dark mop of unruly hair, O'Connor could have easily passed for a priest, if that had been his chosen vocation.

Instead he was wrapped deeply in the fold of the Republican Movement, helping to shape its present into a viable future, a future where, he argued, Ireland would be free to rebuild its shattered economy and take its rightful place amongst the nations of the world. His words offered hope to those who agreed and angst to those who feared the prospect of a return to warfare. There was no in-between.

The Treaty, he told the amassed volunteers, had at its heart a poison so strong that it would rip the country asunder for generations to come if it were allowed to prevail.

Voices raised in objection to the rear of the hall were ignored as he continued his presentation. The Dáil could not, he argued, continue to present the Treaty as a viable option for the future of the Republic with Ulster lying dismembered and in conflict, with brother turning against brother, father against son, as the dream of a true Republic was diluted for personal and political reasons. We must be strong, he urged the volunteers. We must prevail—if not for our sake, then for the sake of unborn generations. For if we, in fear, allow this opportunity to pass us by, we shall never have the chance to make right our wrongs and we will go to our graves knowing that we did not do that which was right, that which was necessary.

As O'Connor's speech came to an end thunderous applause filled the hall, with volunteers cheering and stamping their feet in agreement. O'Connor smiled stiffly, not wanting to show his pleasure at their response. There was still much to be done and many people to win over. It would be a long night.

Liam Mellows and Cathal Brugha were next up, making impassioned pleas for the hearts and minds of the amassed volunteers. Finally, after much discussion, a vote was taken on whether the establishment of a military dictatorship should proceed in the absence of what some Republicans termed real leadership from the Dáil. By only two votes, one of which was Brugha's, the motion to establish a dictatorship fell and the rest of the night was dedicated to the formation of an Executive and an Army Council who, when the time came, could replace the Dáil as a governing body, if necessary.

Jack had voted against the idea of a dictatorship, as had most of the members of his unit. It was, he felt, up to the people to run the country, and not a couple of self-appointed generals, however well meaning they might be.

With the convention coming to a close the lines had been firmly drawn in the sands of time. It was clear, according to Brugha, that no further funding of any description could be expected from the Dáil, and it was time, therefore, to increase their fundraising activities. This meant only one thing—the robbery of banks and post offices, the requisitioning of transport and the raiding of Free State arsenals to fuel what could turn out to be a long military campaign against those in favour of the Treaty, the British Army, or both. Time alone would tell which way Collins and his supporters would go when it came to the final crunch. It would also tell whether the British government under Lloyd George would allow a re-negotiation of the Treaty to take place, or whether they would make an attempt to re-take the country from which they were still in the process of disengaging.

As the noisy crowds shuffled from the auditorium, refuelling arguments and ideals, Jack caught sight of his commanding officer, Seán Fitzpatrick, an honourable, well-spoken man with a great sense of humour and undeniable leadership qualities. Apart from overseeing Jack's unit, he was one of the Dublin Brigade's top men. It had been Seán who got Jack and his cousin Terry, along with another few Fianna na hÉireann boys, into the Brigade a few years before. Since then they had become close friends. Seán smiled openly as he saw Jack and Terry approach.

'How are you lads?' Seán asked.

'We're fine, Seán—yourself?' Jack asked.

'Oh, up to my neck in all of this committee stuff at the moment. I'll be glad when we can make a final decision as to our next move.'

'What do you think that might be?' Terry asked.

'You'll find out soon enough. In the meantime, have a word with some of the lads; tell them that I want the unit together tomorrow night. I have a few plans for you over the next week or so. I'd recommend that you get a good night's sleep tonight—it might be the last you get for a few days,' Seán said with a smile.

'Where are we meeting this time?' Jack asked knowing Seán's habit of dragging them around the city to different meeting places and safe houses.

'The upstairs room in that pub by the four lamps in Rathmines. Nine o'clock should be all right.'

'The lads will be there,' Jack promised.

'I'd best be off. I have another two meetings to attend this evening,' Seán said, checking through a few sheets of paper he held in his hands as he walked away.

'You see. It's starting already. I know there's going to be some action over the next few months. I can feel it in my bones,' Jack said, dragging Terry by the sleeve towards the exit, where they once again met up with Thomas and Barry Murphy.

'We thought you might want to go for a pint,' Barry said, wiping his mouth with obvious thirst.

'Maybe just the one. I've had a chat with Seán—he says he's got a few things for us to be doing over the next couple of days. The unit's meeting up tomorrow night over in Rathmines at around nine.'

'What do you think he has in mind?' Thomas asked.

'I don't know. Maybe a little fundraising,' Jack said with a glint in his eye and a short conspiratorial laugh.

'More withdrawals! I'd never been in a bank until I joined the Dublin Brigade!' Barry said with a smile.

The four men walked purposefully down Dame Street, past Jury's Hotel and rounded the corner by the old Parliament buildings on College Green.

'Where do you want to go?' Thomas asked.

'Conway's, maybe, up on Parnell Street, or Slattery's of Capel Street. I don't mind,' Terry said.

'Conway's?' Barry suggested, waiting for disagreement. There was none.

As they passed the General Post Office, Jack could feel a lump rising in his throat as he always did, when passing the building. The thought of his father, riddled with bullets in the doorway on the day before Pearse surrendered, brought tears and anger flooding through his very being. Tears at the loss of his father, and anger at the way that the Irish Volunteers had been treated by their own people as the Rising was underway. It was only afterwards that the general population's opinion of the insurgents became favourable. The self-sacrificing nature of all involved had spurred on the fight for Irish freedom. Yet again blood sacrifice seemed to be the only way forward. Jack wondered if anything would ever change. If there would ever come a time when people could see the light of freedom without the need for the shedding of blood. He knew that it had to happen one day, but in his heart he feared that it was still many years away.

Terry, in an act of friendship, punched Jack's arm lightly, letting him know that he understood. Jack looked at Terry appreciatively and smiled.

Conway's was buzzing with excitement. It was a popular spot amongst Republicans. The four men had to push their way to the bar, where before long, four creamy pints of porter stood settling.

Terry turned to Jack and whispered in his ear.

'McGinley is over in the corner with some of his cronies. Barry and Thomas will go crazy if they spot him.'

'Well, if it happens, it happens,' Jack said philosophically. 'There's not a lot we can do about it.'

'What are you two whispering about?' Thomas asked, picking up his glass with a palpable reverence.

'Oh, nothing much. Terry just spotted your mate McGinley over in the corner,' Jack said, wondering if he was in the mood for a fight.

'Well he'd better not venture over this way,' Barry said matter-of-factly.

'Forget about it. I'm not in the mood for arguing, lads,' Terry said before lifting his glass to his lips and taking a long sip. The porter left creamy white foam on his upper lip, which he reflexively removed with the back of his hand. 'Let's just have a few pints and forget about it.'

McGinley wandered over with two friends—one of whom Jack immediately recognised as John Maher. He was a brigade member, or at least had been, up until the signing of the Treaty. Since then he had only turned up at occasional meetings—usually when a vote was required. Jack had heard that he had a brother who was now wearing the Free State uniform. This, to Jack, meant only one thing: neither Maher nor McGinley and his other friend, whom Jack didn't recognise, could be trusted.

'Listen,' McGinley said to Thomas, 'let's just forget about what happened earlier all right? It got a little out of hand, that's all.'

'Nothing got out of hand, Mick. You said what you had to say, and so did I. I still stand by what I said,' Thomas said provocatively.

'Mick, maybe you should just leave it be and take your Free Stater friends with you,' Jack said, aiming that particular insult at Maher.

'There's no need for that,' McGinley said. 'Why can't you just face up to the fact that the Treaty is signed and there's nothing else to be done about it. We'll have to get along together eventually.'

'Not while I still have breath left in my body,' Jack said, seeing only traitors to the cause before him.

'Well that may not be for much longer,' John Maher interjected, 'if you go on talking like that.'

Jack rose to the threat. 'If you'd like to do something about it, then go ahead you traitorous bastard.'

With that an empty glass was thrown in Jack's direction, breaking as it hit the bar. Maher quickly followed with a punch to Jack's stomach as the seven men began fighting, the on-looking customers creating something of a ring around them.

Jack's reflexes got into gear and he returned Maher's onslaught with a flurry of punches that saw his opponent slump to the ground, blood oozing from his nose and lips. Both Barry and Thomas had made straight for McGinley, making short work of him, whilst Terry was suffering somewhat from the incessant pounding he was receiving from the third man. Once Jack had finished with Maher he went to Terry's aid. Between the two of them the unknown man was soon on the floor beside Maher.

Listening to the pleas of the barman the four volunteers straightened themselves up and left the bar, smiling broadly as they did, Terry wiping a trickle of blood from his mouth.

'McGinley won't be so free with his opinions in future,' Thomas said. 'I think I broke his jaw!' The four men began laughing loudly as they headed for a small pub on Dorset Street that they might have a quiet and peaceful pint and laugh about the fight in Conway's.

By the time Jack made his way home it was past midnight. He could see an oil lamp burning through the front window of the house as he entered, which told him that his mother, or perhaps Helen, was still awake.

'Is that you Jack?' his mother's voice inquired as he entered the house.

'Are you still up Ma? I thought you'd be gone to bed hours ago.'

'I wanted to hear what happened at the convention.'

'They've set up an Executive and an Army Council. It looks like the Dáil are going to stop supporting the anti-Treaty units.'

'Is that it? They didn't ask you whether you intended to fight on?'

'That was more or less part of the vote on the Executive and Army Council. We've given them the power to replace the Dáil if it comes to that. They just wanted to see if we would back them.'

'So what happens now?'

'That depends on Collins and Griffith. But I think it should be quiet enough for the next while, so don't be worrying too much.'

'Ah, how can I stop worrying and you following your father to an early grave!'

'I'll be all right. You don't need to worry about me, I can look after myself.'

'That's exactly what your father said to me, God rest his poor soul!'

'Don't, Ma. You know you shouldn't talk like that.'

'But it's such a waste of a young life, Jack. Can't you see it? I understand why you want to fight, but for the love of God, can't you see what it's doing to me and your sister, what it's doing to the whole country? We're at one another's throats over this God-forsaken Treaty. It will bring no good, I can tell you now.'

'I know how you feel, but we are so close to getting what we, what Da fought for. It's nearly over, Ma; it's nearly over. One more push and we'll have a Republic. That's all it will take.'

'And how many more lives is the Republic worth?' she asked, looking up at her son through sorrowful, reddened eyes.

'Good night, Ma,' Jack said, kissing his mother's forehead, before climbing the stairs to his bed.

Jack's mother sat silently in the dim light of the oil lamp staring emptily at the picture of her dead husband. She wondered if she might soon be staring at a picture of her son in the same manner.

Seán Fitzpatrick was in fine form the following night in Rathmines as his men gathered around and listened intently to his words. There was a small post office out in Irishtown, near Sandymount, he told them, which needed to be relieved of its takings the following afternoon. The post office employed only one person, the postmaster, who usually opened up at nine-thirty in the morning, he explained. But it wouldn't be until after lunchtime that there would be any amount of money to be had.

'Go down at around two in the afternoon—he should have a few pounds there by then. It should be straightforward. You'll need transport. You might need to make a quick getaway, though I don't foresee any problem. The postmaster is an old man, so be careful not to hurt him. We don't need any more bad press. And then there's the bank,' Seán added, seeing the eyes of the five men light up with interest. It was one thing taking a few pounds from an old postmaster, but a bank raid would mean a little more planning, a little more excitement. And they hadn't had much of that in the last few weeks. 'The bank is on Baggot Street, on the corner of Haddington Road. I want you to hit it at around three in the afternoon, just when they're getting ready to close up for the day. They should have around a hundred pounds in cash, if my intelligence is right. Try to avoid casualties. I don't want any shooting. Apart from the fact that it'll probably be a waste of ammunition, I don't want people turning against us for shooting civilians—understood?' Seán asked.

All five volunteers nodded.

'Who's bringing the guns?' Barry asked.

'Jack, can you go and see Brian Byrnes tonight? I told him that you'd be coming over. He'll have four revolvers for you. I want three men inside on each job and two outside. So only one of you will be going for the cash-the others just need to make sure the coast is clear. You can decide amongst yourselves who does what. Is that okay, Jack?' Seán asked.

'That's fine,' Jack replied. 'Will I take the guns back over to him tomorrow?'

'No, you can hang onto them for the moment—we'll be busy over the next few weeks. Right, organise where you're going to meet up tomorrow while I find the plans of the bank I drew up for you,' Seán said, searching in the brown leather schoolmaster's bag he had at his feet.

'We could meet over by the mill at half-past one,' Thomas suggested.

'That seems fine,' Con Sullivan replied nodding his head.

It was agreed.

Con was a Corkman who had come to Dublin in 1916 and had forgotten to go home. He had a shock of red hair and a powerful frame that, along with his accent, made him stand out amongst his peers. Because of this he wore a cap at all times in an effort to conceal his conspicuous hair and said little. The other volunteer present was Jimmy O'Toole.

Seán unfolded a sheet of brown wrapping paper on which he had drawn a rough map of the bank on Baggot Street. There was only one entrance, which made it easier to secure, but the entrance was on the corner of the crossroads, meaning that there were four directions from which trouble could come. But, as the Civic Guards were still very badly organised and hardly trained, opposition, Seán said, shouldn't be a problem.

'There are four clerks on duty in the bank most days. I suggest you send someone in first to make sure everything is as it should be. We don't want any surprises in there,' he said going over the plans once more.

Once the plans had been carefully studied by all present, Seán stood up and addressed the unit.

'Right, I want the takings delivered to me tomorrow afternoon at the schoolhouse. But I don't want all of you coming over and traipsing through the school—just one of you. Any volunteers?' Seán asked, knowing that it would make the men laugh.

'Do you not have enough volunteers here already?' Jimmy asked with a smile.

'I'll do it,' Barry said, rubbing his hands together pensively. He always took the planning of a raid more seriously than the others did.

'Right—everything is settled then. I'll give Barry a date for our next meeting tomorrow afternoon. Any questions?'

'Is there a guard on the bank?' Con asked.

'There is, but he's unarmed. You'll be able to take him inside with you. It shouldn't be a problem—he's an auld fellah—and my source of information—so don't go hammering the poor man, understand?'

A collective nodding of heads assured Seán that he was fully understood.

'I want you to get out of there as quickly as possible.

Don't forget that the Staters have taken over Beggar's Bush Barracks—they're just up the road. If they hear about the raid you can be sure you'll have a few of them after you,' he added, getting up to leave. 'Head up along the canal towards Rathmines Bridge and down towards Camden Street, back into the city. Split up down there. It'll make it harder for the Staters to find you.'

Placing his bag under his arm and his hat on his head, Seán left the meeting first, soon followed by Barry, Thomas and then the other three, leaving a gap of a few minutes between each departure to avoid suspicion.

Barry and Thomas headed back towards the city centre with Con Sullivan while Jimmy decided to go to see Brian Byrnes with Jack.

Byrnes lived in a tenement building near Thomas Street, which was surrounded by similar run-down houses packed to overflowing with large families. It was a poor area, and noted for the presence of a few brothels, or kips, as the locals called them. There were also a few street-walkers brazenly touting for business in the shadows between the gas lamps. This was the very way of life that Jack had visions of ending for the poor people of Ireland. In his new Ireland, landlords would be held to account, women wouldn't have to sell their bodies to feed their children, and men would be able to get a fair day's pay for a fair day's labour. But that was still a dream.

Byrnes was around fifty, stood with a definite stoop and had almost shoulder-length greying hair, balding from the forehead—something that made him the target of many cruel jokes. But as the man was something of a hermit it didn't bother him all that much. He had done his fair share in 1916 and had, since returning from a British prison in 1917, decided to take something of a back seat in the movement. Because of his trustworthiness it was decided that he might be a good man to hold weapons, a man who wouldn't draw suspicion. Apart from his unusual haircut there was nothing remarkable about the man and that was what made him perfect for the job.

A suspicious man, Byrnes asked that if and when the guns were to be returned, it be by another's hand. Some of his neighbours, while quiet in many respects, he said, would sell him to the highest bidder in a second. Jack understood completely and thanked Byrnes for his help. Byrnes grunted and closed the door on them once they had received what they had come for—a Parabellum and three Webley revolvers, all loaded and with an extra box of cartridges.

Jack could feel the weight of the gunmetal, the smell of the oil, the powder. It reminded him of his childhood, when he helped his father clean his rifle by the fireside all those years ago. Just the touch of the cold gun metal roused feelings of pleasure, of power, of righteousness.

The two volunteers walked carefully homeward, taking pains to avoid Lord Edward Street and Dublin Castle, lest they run into a Free State patrol. Instead, they crossed the Liffey by Wood Quay and headed up through Smithfield Market towards Mary Street, from where it was but a short walk to Gardiner Street and home.

Jimmy said goodnight as they were reaching Summerhill and Jack headed back to his mother's house, the small bag of guns held firmly under his overcoat.

Chapter Three

It was raining and Jack was happy. The bad weather would mean fewer people on the streets, reducing the chances of the unit running into trouble.

Removing the bag of guns from above the water tank in the attic, where he had hidden them the night before, he examined each one in turn, ensuring that the firing mechanisms were functioning correctly and that they were clean. He put the guns back in their hiding place and went down to have breakfast with his mother and sister, who were busy in the kitchen.

'You're finally out of bed!' Helen said, knowing Jack's love of sleeping late.

'What's for breakfast?' Jack asked, ignoring the comment.

'I made a bit of brown bread this morning and there's a rasher in the pan for you,' Jack's mother replied. 'Sit yourself down and I'll bring it over.'

Jack took a seat at the table, feeling his brain throb slightly with the hangover he had as a result of the previous night's drinking. A distinct bruising had also shown up on the lower left side of his ribcage, thanks to John Maher.

'What are you doing today, Jack? Are you going to be around?' Helen asked.

'Why?'

'Oh, I was wondering if you saw Barry last night, and if you'd be seeing him today....'

'Aye, I saw him last night—he said he'd call around today or tomorrow if he had time. We're a bit busy at the moment,' he whispered, hoping that his mother wouldn't hear him. She had never approved of what the brigade now termed 'fundraising'. Daylight robbery is what she called it and she had heard what he said.

'So, you're off to scare the life out of some more poor working people today?' his mother asked.

'We have no choice. Didn't I tell you that the Dáil is removing funding from us? If we don't get some funds together now we'll be stuck when we go back to war,' Jack said.

'So you are going back to war?' Helen asked, unhappily.

'I don't know. We'll have to wait and see. We're being asked to get ready for it, anyway,' Jack admitted, wishing his breakfast would arrive and that the conversation would change.

'Have you not had enough fighting, Jack?' his mother asked, as if she would prefer him to lay down his gun and get a respectable job and life. 'Do you have to keep on at it all the time? It's got to end sometime, you know. You can't keep fighting all your life because your father was killed. I think he'd want you to stop all of this and get married to Kathy.'

'Don't Ma, for God's sake!' Jack exclaimed, rising from the table with a piece of brown bread in his hand, the rasher on top of it. 'It has to be done. That's all there is to it. If there was another way then I'd gladly go down that road, but the Treaty will split this country in two if it's left as it is,' Jack said, leaving the room and heading back upstairs, eating as he went.

'You're as stubborn as your father was,' Jack's mother called after him, secretly proud that he was.

Jack smiled a little to himself on hearing this as he

climbed back up into the attic to get the guns.

A knock came on the back door. Helen opened it quickly. It was Bridie McGovern from the end of the row.

'There's a lorry-load of Civic Guards out on the street. They're searching all the houses,' she said by way of a warning.

'Thanks, Bridie,' Helen said, as Mrs. McGovern ran off down the alley to pass the message on.

Helen rushed up the stairs and called Jack.

'The Guards are searching all the houses on the street,' she said, hearing Jack rummaging around in the attic.

'Keep them busy while I get out of here,' he replied.

A knock came on the front door announcing the arrival of the Civic Guards. Jack closed down the attic cover and made his way across the wooden beams to the attic space of the next house in the row. He continued making his way across until he came to Kathy's family home, where he opened the attic door and climbed down into the house.

Kathy's mother got the fright of her life as Jack's legs dangled in front of her as she emerged from her bedroom.

'Oh holy God!' she exclaimed.

'It's alright Mrs. Cassidy, it's only me, Jack.'

'What in the name of God are you doing up there?' she asked.

'The Civic Guards are searching all the houses on the street, so I thought I'd give them the slip,' he admitted.

'Well you'd better get a move on before they know what you're up to,' she said, beginning to see the funny side of the situation. 'Kathy's downstairs if you want to have a quick word with her.'

'Thanks Mrs. Cassidy. I'm sorry about having to do this,' Jack apologised.

'Don't worry about it, son, sure my husband used to do

that sort of thing all the time with your father, God be good to him. Who do you think it was that made the gaps in the walls of the attics?' she laughed, leading the way downstairs.

Kathy stood at the foot of the stairs in amazement as Jack followed her mother down into the hallway.

'What were you doing up there?' she asked.

'It's an old escape route your father used to use with Jack's father—the Civic Guards are searching all the houses on the street,' Kathy's mother explained matter-of-factly.

Kathy was happy to see Jack, even though she knew he wouldn't be able to stay very long.

Cradling the bag of guns in one arm, he gently ran the back of his free hand across Kathy's cheek. 'I can't stay. I'll be in touch over the next few days though.'

'You'll need a coat,' Mrs. Cassidy said. 'I'll not send you out in that weather without a coat on your back.'

'Thanks Mrs. Cassidy,' Jack said as she handed him a trench coat and hat. 'I'd better be going.'

As soon as her mother's back was turned, Kathy leaned forward and pressed her lips against Jack's. 'Be careful,' she said, 'and remember that I love you'.

Jack smiled as he turned to leave. As he did so, he suddenly understood the fear that his mother had for him, the love she had for him and the pain that she must have gone through when his father was killed. He hoped Kathy didn't feel the same sense of desperation that his mother so obviously did.

Leaving via the back door, he climbed the rear wall and made his way along the alley to the adjoining street from where he could make good his escape.

Wondering why the Guards were searching his street, he made his way out towards the docks, where he could find shelter from the incessant rain before meeting up with the other members of his unit.

The rain had eased off a little by the time Con Sullivan turned up at the mill near the Grand Canal Docks, less than a half mile from their first intended target. Ten minutes later Thomas and Barry Murphy turned up along with Jimmy O'Toole in a rather battered looking Model T Ford. They all looked to be in good spirits.

'Where did you pick up the car?' Jack asked with a smile.

'Oh, some auld eejit left it running outside a house over by Bolton Street, so we decided to bring it with us. It might be handy, you know,' Barry said with more than a hint of sarcasm.

'Did any of you get raided this morning?' Jack inquired wondering if there was a city-wide turnover going on or whether he had been singled out for special attention.

'No,' Con replied. 'Any of you lads?'

None of the other volunteers had been raided, it turned out.

'So what happened?' Jimmy asked.

'Ah, I had to do a runner with the guns. The Guards were banging on our front door,' Jack said nonchalantly.

'You'd better watch yourself tonight,' Barry said. 'You can stay over in our place if you want, until the coast is clear.'

'It was probably McGinley or Maher from last night. I wouldn't put it past them to tell their Free Stater pals you were holding guns or something, just to get back at you,' Jimmy said.

'Well, they didn't get me, so let's forget about it for now,' Jack said, thinking of the work that lay ahead.

The five volunteers sat in the small black car and went over their plans. Jack handed out the weapons and it was agreed that Jimmy would be the bagman on the post office raid, while Con would take care of the cash in the bank.

The rain began to pour from the heavens once more as Barry drove the unit towards Irishtown Post Office, which they reached at twenty past one in the afternoon.

Jack looked across the road at the post office. It was like almost every other sub-post office in the country—small, grubby and not very busy. He wondered why Seán had wanted them to raid such a small place. After all, there couldn't be more than fifty pounds in the cash box, Jack thought, seeing a priest leave the post office and head across the road towards his church.

'Alright then, who's outside, who's inside?' Barry asked.

'I'll stand outside,' Thomas said.

'So will I,' answered Con.

'Right, then it's just you and me, Jack,' Barry said. 'Are you ready with the bag, Jimmy?'

'Aye, I'm ready.'

Barry left the engine running and the five men got out of the car. Thomas and Con took up their positions at the door while Barry, Jack and Jimmy piled inside. Apart from the ageing postmaster, the place was empty.

Jack waved his revolver in the man's face and began to speak.

'This is a raid on behalf of the Irish Republican Army. If you don't resist you won't be hurt. Now, hand over all the cash you have on the premises,' Jack said, repeating the lines he had learned from Seán, who believed that those being robbed should know where the money was going.

Barry cocked the Webley he was holding and pointed it directly at the old man behind the counter. At the same time Jimmy jumped over and began to rifle the cash drawers, stuffing what he could find into the small bag he was carrying. The postmaster stood silent and still as the men carried out the raid. Only the look in his eyes told the volunteers that he was angry.

'Up the Republic!' Jimmy shouted as he jumped back over the counter.

Within three minutes all five volunteers were back in the car and heading out towards Sandymount Strand where they would count the money and prepare for the next raid.

'That was easy,' Jimmy said, almost disappointed.

'Well, it's better than having a truck full of Staters after us,' Con said with a laugh.

'Sure they can't shoot straight—they wouldn't be any trouble at all, boy,' Thomas said, mocking Con's Cork accent. Con gave him a soft dig in the ribs.

'Right lads, listen,' Jack said. 'I think one of us should go into the bank to have a look around before we go running in with the guns. Who wants to do it?'

Jack had been in a bank raid during the Tan War where an off-duty CID man, who was carrying a gun, happened to be cashing a cheque. Before Jack knew what was happening the man had unholstered his weapon and fired two rounds at one of the three volunteers in the bank, killing him instantly. Jack's reflexes prompted him to lift his right arm, level the gun barrel at the CID man's face and pull the trigger. The man fell like a sack of stones from the crest of a bridge; his head split open by the force of the bullet.

Jack didn't want to go through a similar situation again. It had been hard telling the dead volunteer's mother that her eighteen year old son wasn't coming home and it was the first time he had killed someone at close range.

'Good idea,' Jimmy said, aware of Jack's thoughts.

'I'll go in,' Con said

Thomas counted the money from the post office and Jack went over the plans for the bank raid as they sat looking out over Dublin Bay. The wind was whipping up the waves and dark clouds hovered on the horizon, bearing the weight of fresh rain.

'So, you're going for the cash, Con, I'll go inside—who else wants to go in?' Jack asked, feeling somewhat calmed by the sight and smells of the sea.

'I'll go in this time,' Thomas said.

'Right, that leaves Barry and Jimmy on the door. Con, give Jimmy your gun.'

'We got around forty-five pounds from the post office,' Thomas said, stuffing the money back into the bag.

'That's not so bad. But we should get a lot more in the bank,' Jack said. 'What time is it?'

'Just gone two o'clock,' Barry said, checking his pocket watch.

'Well, we've got over an hour. I think we should drop Con off in the next half-hour to have a look around. We can park on the corner of Percy Place and wait for him. We go in at around three, agreed?' Jack asked. A succession of nods told him they were all in agreement.

Barry started the car and headed away from the strand towards Sandymount Avenue, which would take the five volunteers in towards Upper Baggot Street and the bank. The further they got from Irishtown, the better. The place was sure to be swarming with Civic Guards by now.

Jack wondered why some volunteers had decided to support the Treaty and joined the newly formed Civic Guards. How could a man fight an enemy for six years or more and then just give up at the very moment that persistence would make a difference or win the war, he wondered. It truly baffled him. He remembered the joy he felt when he first joined the Dublin Brigade, how committed and strong in his ideals he was. Seán Fitzpatrick had introduced him to Commandant Oscar Traynor, the man who controlled the entire Dublin Brigade, and Jack was so excited that he had difficulty in finding the words to express himself. Traynor was a decent man. He had asked Jack why he wanted to join the Republican Army. Jack, searching frantically for his voice finally told Traynor that it was in his blood; that his father had been in the GPO in 1916 and he hadn't come out alive. It was, he said, partly for his father, but mostly for himself. Traynor asked what his father's name was, and when Jack told him, Traynor smiled as if he knew the name.

'You're welcome to join the Dublin Brigade, Jack Larkin. Let's hope you're as good a man as your father was,' Traynor had said, clapping him on the back with the flat of his hand and nodding to Seán Fitzpatrick with approval. 'It's more like this one we need.'

Jack remembered Traynor's words. He was proud to be a volunteer and he wouldn't give up hope of achieving the Republic. There was no way he would settle for less than a thirty-two county Irish Republic free from outside interference and control—despite what some of the other volunteers had said in recent months. It was as if it was all coming down to personalities rather than politics and that troubled him greatly. He had heard grown men saying 'I'm a Dev man, and I'll go whichever way he does,' and others saying the same thing about Collins and other leaders. Some men seemed happy to just follow their commanding officers, largely ignorant of the bigger political picture, but sure in the knowledge that they were doing their best for Ireland.

Jack began to question his own reasons for fighting. Were they as pure as he thought? Was it partly a need for revenge? Was it the guilty feeling he had whenever he looked at the photograph of his father? Was it for a Republic he was fighting, for the people of Ireland, for social change and autonomy? Sometimes he didn't know which of these feelings was the strongest, which were the backbones of his idealism. He only knew that he must fight with all of his conviction and courage. He knew that he had to carry on where his father had left off—to fan the flames from which the fledgling nation would rise like a phoenix from the ashes. He couldn't stop now.

Barry parked the old Model T Ford around the corner from the bank, off Haddington Road and Con went to have a look inside. As he approached the door he saw the security guard. He was a youngish man, no more than thirty, and not the old man that Seán had spoken of. Taking a cigarette from his pocket, Con stopped beside the guard and smiled.

'I don't suppose you'd have a light there, would you?' Con asked, by way of starting a conversation.

'Certainly,' the security guard replied cordially, removing a box of matches from his tunic pocket.

'Thanks,' Con said, lighting his cigarette and the returning the matches. 'You're not the same fellah they have on the door most days, are you?' Con asked.

'Oh, the man who's supposed to be working today fell off his bicycle yesterday and hurt his head. I think he was on his way home from the pub,' the guard joked.

'Aye, you have to watch yourself after a few pints,' Con agreed with a smile, before entering the bank to have a look around.

It was quiet inside the bank, with no more than three customers seeing to their business at the counter. Con's eyes scanned the entire room once, before he noticed that a bank clerk was asking him if he could be of any assistance.

'Yes,' Con replied, reaching into his inside pocket as if to get a savings book.

'Do you have an account here?' the teller asked.

'Yes,' Con replied, 'but I don't seem to have my savings book with me. I must have left it in the car. I'll be back in a minute,' he said with a smile.

The bank teller nodded sharply and returned his gaze to a sheet of paper that was filled with numbers and boxes. Con stepped outside and headed for the car.

'Well?' Barry asked. 'Is it all easy enough?'

'There's a different guard on the door—it's a younger man than Seán said. But the bank layout is pretty straight-forward—four cashiers with their own cash drawers. There's hardly anyone in there—I think we should do it now,' Con said, feeling the adrenaline begin to pulse through his veins.

'Right,' Jack said, 'let's get this over with as quickly as possible—and we don't want any shooting—remember what Seán said.'

'Do you think we should stay in the car?' Barry asked.

'Yeah, you stay in the car, Barry. Jimmy, you stand out-side the bank—don't let anyone in. We'll take the guard inside, so there shouldn't be a problem,' Jack said, getting out of the car, following Thomas and Con back to the bank.

Con smiled at the security guard as he approached and the guard smiled back. Grabbing him suddenly by the throat, Con dragged him into the bank as Barry and Jimmy pulled up outside. Jack and Thomas entered the bank behind Con, waving their guns in the air.

'This is a raid by the Irish Republican Army. If you don't resist you won't be hurt,' Jack shouted, as Con threw the security guard to the floor, Thomas keeping him covered with his revolver. 'Stand away from your cash drawers and don't do anything stupid. All we want is the money,' Jack added, seeing the terror in the eyes of a young woman behind the old wooden counter.

Con climbed over the counter and began to fill a money-bag with the contents of the cash drawers. It seemed like an awful lot of money, Con thought, moving from drawer to drawer with speed.

Once the security guard had found the nerve he stood up and tried to grab Jack's revolver. Jack pushed the man away and hit him across the back of the head with his gun. The guard collapsed in a heap on the floor and stayed put.

'Come on, will you!' Thomas said, growing agitated.

'I'm almost done,' Con replied emptying the last drawer and jumping back over the counter.

'Let's go!' Jack shouted, as the three men made for the door.

Thomas slipped on the wet footpath, dropping his revolver. It discharged as it hit the ground, attracting the attention of passers-by. Picking up the revolver he hurled himself into the back of the car. Barry drove off towards Rathmines Bridge, where they had agreed to ditch the car and split up.

'What the hell were you thinking, Thomas?' Jack asked as the car sped alongside the canal. 'Why did you have your gun cocked?'

'Just in case there was any . . .'

'Look, never mind, just give me the guns. Barry, you're taking the money over to Seán, aren't you?'

'That's right.'

'Well, take a pound out of it, we'll go for a drink tonight. I think we've earned it,' Jack said, exhaling loudly in an effort to calm himself down. They ditched the car and split up. Thomas and Con headed for a pub on Camden Street, while Barry headed up to Seán Fitzpatrick's schoolhouse to drop off the money. Jack and Jimmy, having arranged to met the lads later that evening, decided to head over to Jimmy's place where they could store the guns.

As they walked down through the city centre, Jack, whose mind had been fixed on the question of his own idealism asked Jimmy why he was fighting.

'Because it's the right thing to do,' Jimmy said, blankly.

'Yeah, but you know, after all of the talk that's been going on over the last few months, what with the Treaty and so many volunteers going over to Collins' side. I was just wondering why you think it's right to fight on. I'm not questioning your will, just wondering what your reasons are,' Jack said, as delicately as possible. He had yet to meet a volunteer who wouldn't swing for you if he thought you doubted his commitment.

'You've known me long enough for that,' Jimmy said, slightly surprised at the question. They had fought together during the Tan War and never before had such a question raised its ugly head.

'I know. It's just that I was trying to answer that question for myself and I thought it was difficult to put a finger on the exact reason—it's more like a lot of reasons, all jumbled up together, both personal and political. It's not just a hatred of what the British have done to our people, it's a desire to make us stronger, better. Do you understand what I'm getting at?' Jack asked.

Jimmy had never heard Jack speak like this in all the years that they had known each other. They had first met in their teenage years while members of Fianna na hÉireann, under the command of Liam Mellows. They had become friends almost immediately and had maintained their friendship throughout the war, having joined the IRA on the same day. Jimmy wondered if Jack was having second thoughts about continuing the struggle for the

Republic. He had always been so sure of his reasons in the past and Jimmy had never seen fit to question them.

'I'm not sure that I do understand,' Jimmy admitted.

'Well, part of me is doing this for Ireland, for the good of the people. Another part of me is doing it for myself and Kathy I suppose and then there's a part of me that is just seeking revenge for the death of my father,' Jack said, hoping Jimmy would understand.

'So what's the question?'

'I'm just interested in why you want to continue fighting—it can be a difficult question to answer,' Jack said, hoping that his friend would agree.

'I don't know,' Jimmy said, shrugging his shoulders, 'maybe it's because of people like you—friends and family that are involved. Don't get me wrong, I want to see an Irish nation and I want the English out of the country for good, but it's more of a family tradition in my case. I've been brought up with it, you know. It's almost expected of me. My grandfather was an IRB man and my father was in the Irish Volunteers. It's in my blood. It's as though the only reason I exist is to fight for Irish freedom. I know it sounds silly, but I truly believe that I have a duty to do as much as I can,' Jimmy said, almost shocked that he could describe his reasons for fighting in so clear a manner. 'It's like I was born to do this, and nothing else.'

Both volunteers fell silent for a few moments as they crossed over the Liffey, seeing Nelson's Pillar rise like a phallus from the heart of Dublin City. It was as if the English were mocking them with their military might and accomplishment. But to most Irishmen, Nelson merely stood there as a reminder of a job yet to be done.

Entering Jimmy's lodgings on Charles Street, off Mountjoy Square, Jack looked around cautiously to make sure they weren't being followed. They climbed three sets of stairs and Jimmy unlocked the door that kept him safe from the outside world.

The sound of children screaming came from the rooms below, followed by loud, angry voices and the slamming of a door. There were six families living in the building, a three storey Georgian house that had been left to decay. The sash windows were rotting in their frames and the doors barely hung on their hinges.

Jimmy's room was no more than a storage space with a bed in it. He didn't even have a cooker. He washed from a bucket of cold water that stood in the corner of the room. Jack felt sorry for his friend. He had often asked why he didn't just move home instead of renting the room. Jimmy's response to this question was simple: freedom. He liked to be able to come and go as he pleased and invite whomever he wished to join him. There was no way he could bring a girl home with him if he was living with his mother and there was definitely no way he could get them into bed, he had said with a smile. Jack could see the sense of it, having longed to be alone with Kathy now for months. It was practically impossible for them to get time alone and when they did, it was usually in public places— not the best situation for intimate contact.

Jimmy took the bag of guns from Jack and hid them under the floorboards, being careful not to make too much noise, lest the people below hear what he was doing.

'I'd offer you a cup of tea, but I don't have any,' Jimmy laughed.

'Don't worry. It's not tea I've a taste for right now,' Jack said, rubbing his jaw.

'Well, I do have a little left in a bottle here somewhere,' Jimmy said, getting down on his hands and knees and searching under the bed. Producing a quarter bottle of whiskey he smiled and handed the bottle to Jack who uncorked it and drank deeply until it burned his throat and brought tears to his eyes.

'Jaysus, that hits the spot every time!' Jack said, rubbing his stomach as the warmth of whiskey made its presence known.

'Give it here to me and let me do a little damage to myself,' Jimmy said, taking the bottle from Jack and drinking heartily from it.

'A job well done, eh?' Jack said.

'A job well done!' Jimmy agreed.

Chapter Four

The five volunteers met up later that evening in a small pub on Dorset Street. Barry, who had delivered the money to Seán Fitzpatrick, said that they had been given further orders and that Seán himself would turn up a little later to go through what was next on their list of priorities.

A total of two hundred pounds had been raised in the day's activities, Barry said, and Seán had told him to take two pounds out of that and split it up between the unit for drinks or whatever else was needed. The volunteers smiled on hearing this. You could get a small army drunk on two pounds and that is exactly what they were.

'What else did he say,' Jimmy asked, wondering if there was anything big in the air.

'Well, he asked me not to say anything,' Barry said. 'But he'll be here in a while to tell you himself.'

'More fundraising?' Thomas asked

'I think we've done enough fundraising for one week,' Con said.

'We're going to move in the next few days,' Barry said, unable to contain himself any longer. 'That's all I'm telling you. Seán will fill in the blanks.'

Moving in the next few days, Jack thought. It sounded very much like something big was on the cards. And if that were the case then they would have to get more arms and ammunition together.

A lot of the brigade's arms had fallen into Free State

hands over the last few months, with most of the Dublin-based former British Army barracks being handed over to pro-Treaty units from around the country. An attempt to retrieve some of those arms was probably what Seán had in mind.

Jack had taken part in this sort of operation before and they were always fraught with danger. Barracks and arsenals were usually well protected and attacking them posed a real threat to life and limb. Just one shot fired in anger and all hell could break loose. It had happened the last time that they raided an army barracks. Around thirty volunteers had taken part in the well-orchestrated raid on Portobello Barracks in Rathmines two years earlier. Timing was important, as the majority of those serving on the base had been sent out to deal with an incident in the city centre—an incident that was caused by another group of volunteers setting fire to shops and shooting dead an off-duty soldier. A skeleton crew remained at the barracks and although well armed, they were no match for the thirty volunteers.

In no time at all they had loaded a tender with rifles, revolvers, mines and ammunition and had driven out the front gates. Two volunteers had died in the raid, but it was still considered a major success. The raid left the Dublin Brigade well armed for the following twelve months. But a raid these days would be a different matter altogether. It would be their first action against their old comrades-in-arms and that would prove difficult, Jack thought, wondering if he could shoot another Irishman.

The five volunteers were just starting their second pint when Seán arrived, smiling as usual.

'Lads,' he said, 'you did a great job today.'

The volunteers smiled like children. It was always nice to receive a compliment from your commanding officer.

'Barry was saying that you have some more work for us?' Jimmy said, hoping Seán would get down to the nitty-gritty as soon as possible. Seán could see the anxious looks in the eyes of the volunteers and decided to play on it for a while.

'I'll get myself a pint, I think,' Seán said.

'Sit down, Seán, I'll get it for you,' Barry said, getting up. 'You can fill them in—they've been doing nothing but asking me questions since I arrived,' Barry laughed.

'And you wouldn't tell them a thing?' Seán asked, knowing only too well that he wouldn't say a word—even to his own brother. Barry smiled and went up to the bar.

'Well, Seán, what's next?' Con inquired, asking the question that was on the lips of all the volunteers.

'Well, tomorrow, six units of the Dublin Brigade are going over to Beggar's Bush Barracks to make a small withdrawal,' Seán said.

'The barracks?' Jimmy asked. 'But Collins' men have already taken that over, haven't they?'

'That's right. But the Brits left behind a good deal of arms and explosives that we'll need,' Seán added, tantalisingly.

'For what?' Jack asked.

'We're going to seize a number of buildings around the city in the next day or so,' Seán said, quietly.

'Which ones?' Thomas asked.

'I can't tell you that just now. But once the Beggar's Bush raid has been successful you'll be told where you're going. So if you have any friends, family or girlfriends you'd like to see,' Seán said, looking directly at Jack, 'you'd best see them tonight, because you may not see them again for quite a while.'

'Is it starting?' Con asked.

'I don't really know. There's still a lot of talking going on. Everything could change overnight as far as I'm concerned. I've been told that Collins is behind the campaign in Ulster at the moment and that he's even armed some of our lads up there, so I don't really know what's going to happen. We'll have to sit tight and see,' Seán admitted.

'So do you think it will be hard getting into Beggar's Bush?' Jimmy asked. 'How many men do they have there now?'

'Ah, only twenty or thirty—most of them go home to their families in the evening and they're not expecting this. Besides, a few of the lads are coming back over to our side, so it shouldn't be too messy,' Seán said, with hope in his heart.

'What time are we going in?' Thomas asked, as Barry handed Seán his pint.

'Late tomorrow night. We'll meet on Wexford Street and head over by Ranelagh Bridge. Can one of you get an open truck of some description? We'll need it to carry both the men and the arms,' Seán asked.

'I'll get it,' Barry said.

Barry always got the transport. It was almost expected of him at this stage, but Seán never took anything for granted—another reason why the men liked him.

'Who else is coming along—what other units?' Jimmy asked.

'Around five or six units are supposed to show up—everyone from the south city to Drumcondra, yourselves, the lads from the Liberties and some lads from over by Smithfield—there's going to be over thirty of you,' Seán said. 'We'll be meeting up just before, so we can all go at the same time. It shouldn't be a problem.'

'What sort of arms and ammo do they have in the Bush Barracks?' Con asked.

'The usual sort of stuff—old RIC carbines, Mauser bolt-actions, Canadian Ross Rifles, Lee Speeds and hopefully a few short-mag Lee-Enfield MIIIs—they're a great little rifle,' Seán said.

'What about short arms?' Barry asked.

'I don't know—but they should have some of the old Parabellums we got a few years ago, maybe some Browning LEs and Smith & Wesson revolvers. If you're very lucky you might be able to get your hands on a Mauser machine pistol or two. They're great yokes altogether,' Seán said, trying to encourage his men to go for the good stuff.

'And some Mills Bombs and mines as well, I suppose?' Jack added.

'Aye, and as much ammo as we can get our hands on. I'm not sure, but I think there may be a few raids planned—but this is the only one you'll be involved in, so make it worthwhile. You'll need every piece you can lay your hands on and I don't want to hear people complaining afterwards that they didn't have a chance to get a hold of something decent, do ye hear me?' Seán said.

Once the meeting point had been arranged the six men parted company and went their own ways. If they were going to launch a full-scale raid on a protected army barracks and then take over some key city centre buildings they would be on duty for the foreseeable future. That usually meant poor rations, bad sleeping arrangements, cold, draughty places and the prospect of catching a bullet. It was at times like this that the men withdrew, went crazy on the drink, or went quietly home, contemplating their intended actions and psyching themselves up so they could get the job done. Fear had to be put to one side, courage brought to the fore and what some might regard as a band of ill-trained and ragged men in trench coats would become a functioning unit inseparable in thought and deed. Five pairs of eyes acting as one, each volunteer looking out for the next. It was an irresistible bond.

Jack's unit, with all of its present members, had been together for over a year and a half now without a loss. They had been in some pretty hairy situations in that time, having to shoot their way out on more than one occasion. It was this pressure under fire that brought the men closer. They were more than brothers to one another—they were a living, breathing and functioning organism—each with his own separate role, which, when combined, made them as strong as they had thus far needed to be in order to survive and to be effective. That was all their commanding officers could ask of them.

Jack made his way home through the quieter streets. The weather had turned foul again and the rain was coming down with renewed vigour, sending rivulets of dirty water rushing down the dark streets into overflowing gutters and drains. The streets were empty and therefore safe.

On entering the house via the back lane, Jack's mother put the kettle on the range and took the wet overcoat and hat from him, hanging them over a chair near the fire.

'Did the Civic Guards say what they were looking for?' Jack asked

'No, they didn't say anything—they didn't even ask for you by name this time,' his mother said.

'What did they say?'

'I think it was just a random raid. You know, the kind of thing the RIC were doing last year,' she said. ' I shouldn't worry too much about it. Are you all right?'

'I'm fine.'

'We heard about the post office and bank this afternoon. Was that you?' Helen asked.

'Yeah. Everything went fine and no one was hurt.'

'But shots were fired, according to the evening papers,' Helen said, worried that Barry might be hurt.

'That was Thomas—he slipped on his way out of the bank.'

'But no one was hurt?'

'Everyone's fine. Barry was asking for you. He said he'd call around, only we've got a lot to do in the next few days. I think we're going to be kept busy,' Jack said.

'Are you going to be away for a few days?' his mother asked.

'I think so.'

'Well I'll put a bag of food and clothes together for you. You might need them,' she said, knowing full well that he would need them and would be very grateful for them in the coming days. By now she had learned that Jack always understated what he was about to do. If he said he was going away for a few days, that meant he didn't know how long he would be gone.

'Is Barry going with you?' Helen asked.

'He is,' Jack said.

'Tell him I was asking for him,' she said, trying to hide the fear in her voice.

'Are you hungry?' Jack's mother asked.

'I'm so hungry I could eat a Protestant,' Jack said, making the two women smile. 'Do you mind if I just go over to see Kathy for a while?' Jack asked, knowing that his mother would start cooking straight away.

'Be back in a half hour—I'll have a plate of spuds and cabbage for you,' she said, giving him the coat and hat to take back with him.

'Thanks Ma,' Jack said with a warm smile.

Kathy was thrilled to see Jack, and her mother was happy to have her husband's coat and hat back in one piece.

Getting up from her place at the kitchen table once pleasantries had been exchanged, Kathy's mother left the two young lovebirds with a small warning.

'I'll be in the next room if you want anything,' she said, meaning that she'd hear everything they did, so they had better do nothing they'd be ashamed of.

Kathy sat opposite her young man at the kitchen table and gripped his hand tightly. She had done this many times over the last few years. He knew she was afraid of what was to come, and if the truth were to be known, so was he. Having faced death on more than one occasion in the line of duty, Jack was all too aware of how easy it would be to stand up at the wrong moment or lose concentration for a split second and catch a bullet. He had been wounded once in the past, but it was merely a flesh wound. A bullet had ripped through the muscle of his upper arm, going in straight, but coming out sideways, leaving an ugly scar. A few inches to the right and he could have been dead. It was such moments that brought home the sheer frailty of the human body—how easily it could be broken and torn asunder. Kathy's fears were real and for perhaps the first time, Jack was becoming acutely aware of them. It felt good knowing someone cared so much about you—that they worried all of the time. But then he knew it would break her heart if he was killed.

'What do you think is going to happen?' Kathy asked, fighting back her tears. 'It's definitely war again, isn't it? I wish it could be all over and we could just be together,' she said, squeezing his hand tightly again and gazing intently at his unshaven face. His eyes sparkled like sunlight on water, full of compassion, full of knowledge, full of life. She loved him with more strength than she loved life itself and she knew she would do anything for him.

'We'll have plenty of time together,' Jack said, in an

effort to reassure her.

'And we'll be married in the spring, like you promised?'

'Yes, and we'll go down to Kerry on our honeymoon. Sure I'm already saving up for it,' Jack said, thinking of the five pounds he had hidden away in the attic. 'We'll have the best wedding our street has ever seen and a party with cakes and food and lots to drink and we'll invite everyone we've ever met. We'll have the best party you could ever imagine.'

'It will be like that, won't it Jack?'

'Of course it will, sweetheart, of course it will. Have I ever let you down?'

'No,' she said, looking down at his roughened hands.

'Well, I won't let you down this time, either,' he said, caressing her face with his free hand and kissing her softly on the lips. 'I love you with all of my heart and I want you to be my wife. We'll have a great life together, you'll see.'

'I wish all of this was over and done with,' she said, a tear running down her cheek.

'It's almost over, darling, it's almost over. Maybe another few months, that's all. It'll soon straighten itself out. Wait and see. By the end of the summer we'll be laughing about this moment thinking how foolish we were,' he said, wiping the tear away with his fingers.

'But what if something happens to you?'

'I'll be fine. I've got the best of the brigade behind me and I know what I'm doing. Don't worry darling. I'll be fine. I promise,' he said, kissing her once again and feeling the grip of her hand.

'I wish we could be alone together,' Kathy said, looking into his eyes. 'Just you and me, with no one to disturb us.'

'I know. Soon, Kathy, I promise. We'll be together soon,' Jack said getting up to go.

He remembered the first time he had kissed her. They were only twelve and were playing catch and kiss in the street. Kathy had allowed herself to be caught by no one else, so Jack kept chasing her. His friends had made fun of him for weeks afterwards, but he didn't mind. Just the chance to kiss such a pretty girl was worth all of the teasing in the world. They had become friends and were walking out together by their fourteenth year. That was almost ten years ago now and Jack remembered how kind she had been to him when his father was killed. No one else understood like she did, no one could feel the pain like she did.

'Do you have to go?' Kathy asked.

'I do. I'll try to call around again as soon as I can. Thank your mother again for the coat, will you? And take care of yourself my darling girl,' Jack said kissing her full lips once more before leaving.

Kathy stood in the doorway as Jack made his way down the lane and back into his mother's house. She felt empty, afraid and lonely. Nothing seemed to make any sense when he wasn't there. It was as if nothing else mattered, only Jack and Kathy, Kathy and Jack.

Jack's unit met up in Wexford Street, or the Dardenelles, as it had become known during the Tan War, due to its popularity as an ambush spot. It was there that Barry had arranged to meet them with an open-topped truck. Seán was also coming along on the raid and had brought an extra revolver in case it was needed.

The six men, all in reasonably good spirits, climbed into the truck and headed out towards Ranelagh Bridge, as arranged. From there, Seán told the volunteers, they would head over to Beggar's Bush along the canal and down Haddington Road to the barracks, while the other units would approach from different streets. Over thirty well armed volunteers were heading straight for the arsenal with one thing in mind—getting their hands on the best equipment there was.

The cool April breeze seemed even sharper that night with the darkness of cloud hanging overhead, threatening more rain.

The truck bounced over the potholes in the road toward its destination, attracting the attention of the few people who were still out on the streets. It was obvious that the lorry-load of volunteers were intent on creating some form of havoc, somewhere.

The IRA had been patrolling the streets since the truce was signed and had been carrying their weapons openly. But in the recent past, with the indecision that was in the air, the number of patrols had fallen and open weapon carrying had become less common. This made the lorry full of men more conspicuous.

One or two passers-by shouted support to them, whilst others shook their heads in dismay, wishing the whole episode in recent Irish history would just go away. Some people were even wishing the British would come back and bring a little stability to the country, which seemed to be teetering ever closer to civil war. But the majority knew that the only way forward was the way in which they were presently heading as difficult as it seemed.

The volunteers checked their revolvers as the truck made its way along Haddington Road, catching sight of four other trucks as they pulled up a short distance from the barracks entrance, waiting for a signal to move. When the signal finally came, Barry headed for the barracks gate and drove straight through it, much to the surprise of the soldier on duty, who brought his rifle up to stop the intruders. The sharp crack of an automatic pistol from on board the second lorry saw the soldier fall to the ground clutching his thigh whilst attempting to scramble to safety. The fourth truck stopped briefly as it entered the barracks yard, with five men getting off to secure the gate.

Barry headed straight for the arsenal as rifle fire filled the air, shattering the windscreen of the truck. The volunteers returned fire, their attackers fleeing for cover as the men in the second truck opened up with their rifles. It was obvious that there were only ten or so men at the barracks and they were no match for the thirty volunteers. The gunfire quickly subsided as Barry reached the arsenal, stopping the lorry by the doorway. There, waiting for them with the key, was a Free State soldier with a smile on his face.

'I've been waiting for you for over a half an hour. Where have you been?' he asked, half jokingly.

Seán shook his head and took the keys from the man.

'If you're coming with us I'd suggest you get that uniform off you before the lads rip it off,' he said.

The soldier smiled and followed the volunteers into the storeroom.

Jack's eyes opened wide with delight upon seeing the array of weapons now at their disposal. Grabbing the first magazine-loaded short arm he could find, a Browning LE, he stuffed it into his pocket before grabbing five brand new short-magazine Lee Enfield MIIIs that he carried out to the lorry. Each volunteer did the same until all of the rifles were gone. The next truck pulled up to get the explosives and ammunition boxes. It took fifteen minutes to empty the arsenal and load the trucks.

'Where to now?' Barry asked, looking at Seán.

'The Four Courts,' Seán said with a smile. 'We're taking over the Four Courts.'

The volunteers looked at each other in amazement for a few seconds until it occurred to one of them to speak.

'How many are coming with us?' Con asked, hoping that there would be a damned sight more men going to court today than there were present.

'Don't worry—who do you think all of this is for?' Seán said. 'There's over two hundred.'

'What other buildings are being taken?' Jack asked.

'Kilmainham Gaol, a few buildings on O'Connell Street, the Kildare Street Club and a few other spots around the town,' Seán replied.

'What do you think Collins is going to do when he hears this?' Jimmy asked.

'I don't know. He's still talking with Rory O'Connor and the Executive, so time will tell.'

'So you don't think they'll attack the Courts?' Jack asked.

'I doubt it. Still, we've got to get the place secured, just in case,' Seán said. 'Now get a move on and let's get going.'

Jack wondered just what seizing the Four Courts and other strong points around the city might actually achieve. Over the last number of years he had learned that the ability to strike hard at the British establishment and to disappear into the background was the IRA's strength. But by taking buildings and attempting to seize key areas of the city they were leaving themselves open to attack from all sides—either by the British, if they should come back into the fray, or by pro-Treaty troops.

It was a move that didn't inspire confidence, he thought, wondering where it might lead. Practically all of the Dublin Brigade were anti-Treaty, and that would be upwards of a thousand men, a formidable force, as most would be willing to fight on to the end. But stationary warfare was not their strongpoint. It remained to be seen what the Executive leaders had in mind. Perhaps it was just an attempt to put pressure on the Dáil to come around to the Executive's way of thinking, to reassess their line on the Treaty. Whatever they had in mind, Jack had a bad feeling about it that grew stronger as the lorry neared the Four Courts.

Jack's view didn't appear to be the common one. All of the other volunteers seemed truly excited at the thought of making the move. Jack was not in the mood to discuss the pros and cons at present. They had a job to do and that was that. If it was what the leadership wanted, then that's what they would get.

Jack removed the Browning LE pistol from his trench coat pocket and ran his hands over its smooth body. It was brand new and had probably never been fired. He could feel the thin layer of oil that covers new weapons as he handled it. Removing the magazine, he grabbed a handful of bullets from an open ammo box and filled his pockets before slowly filling up the magazine and clicking it back into place. It was a lovely gun.

'Right,' Seán said, trying to get the attention of the volunteers. 'We'll be taking the east wing of the building along with another twenty or thirty men. I'll be in charge of our section, so if there's any trouble, just come to me,' Seán said. 'The first thing we have to do is store the explosives and ammo in the cellars. We want no civilians left in the place, understand? Then I want you to barricade the windows in our section—but don't go breaking any glass. There'll be time enough for that if and when it's necessary—besides, it's still cold out these nights and you'll be sleeping on the floor—so think ahead.'

'How long are we here for?' Jimmy asked.

'No date has been given to me. But as this is our new headquarters I've a feeling we'll be here for the foreseeable future, so make yourselves at home,' Seán replied.

'What about the other buildings we've taken over?' Thomas asked.

'They will be holding their posts just like we are,' Seán said.

'So it's a question of wait and see?' Jack asked.

'More or less. It's up to the Executive and the politicians to find a suitable way forward. If they can't, then we are the only possible way forward left open to the country,' Seán replied. 'And we won't let them down, sure we won't lads?' The volunteers agreed as the convoy of open-topped lorries made their way down along the banks of the Liffey towards the Four Courts.

Sixty or seventy men could be seen across the river heading towards the courthouses, rifles on their shoulders, preparing to meet their comrades-in-arms on the steps of the Four Courts. Excitement filled the air.

Chapter Five

There was no opposition to the volunteers who stormed the Four Courts. They had full possession of the buildings in a matter of minutes, transferring their equipment and stores into the cellars, where they would be relatively safe from damage, should anyone choose to attack.

As Seán had instructed, the twenty or so men stationed in the east wing of the courts settled in. They were glad to see that the comrades they had seen proudly marching down the quays had blankets with them. All they needed now was a reliable food supply and they could hold the buildings indefinitely, Jack thought. And as Smithfield Market was located right behind the Four Courts, there would be more than enough food to feed the garrison.

It didn't take long for news of the arms' seizures around Dublin to reach Dáil Eireann, where protests were aimed at Collins, who was given responsibility for seeing the matter was brought to a speedy and peaceful end. But as it presently stood, Rory O'Connor, Ernie O'Malley and Liam Mellows sat back comfortably listening to gramophone records and drinking tea in the Law Library on the day of the seizures, waiting for the inevitable furore that their actions would cause.

O'Connor's plans for the volunteers present were simple: he wanted them to requisition as many trucks and buses as possible whilst also ensuring they had a good supply of petrol. Apart from that, bank and post office 'withdrawals' were also set to continue over the coming days, with the

Four Courts being held as their main base.

O'Connor's intention, Seán told Jack, was to send some volunteers up to help the Northern Command re-take the six counties, whilst maintaining a firm grip on Dublin's heart. Jack thought the plan ambitious. Seán was inclined to agree. It was a plan that never really got off the ground.

Even stranger still, after less than a week in their new-found home, the volunteers were asked to pile all of their old Tan War arms on the back of a small truck. They were instructed to only keep their recently acquired guns. Questions were raised though answers were not provided. But one volunteer, a man by the name of Seán Lemass, saw a Free State soldier drive the truck away, having delivered another filled with a similar number of new weapons. No one quite knew what was happening, but word eventually filtered down that Collins, who was still behind much of the Republican resistance in the north, had asked O'Connor for his old arms in exchange for new ones. The plan was to equip the northern brigades with the older guns. That way, if captured, the guns would not leave a trail leading back to Collins, most of whose men were now carrying top of the range weaponry that had been left behind, or recently delivered to the Irish government by the British. Any connection with the ongoing actions in the north would lead to an immediate breakdown in the relationship that Collins was maintaining with Lloyd George. And that could mean all-out war.

The situation was beginning to get extremely complicated, with delegations of men coming and going and meetings taking place at all hours of the day and night in the courthouses. At one point it appeared that the anti-Treaty troops and the Free Staters might rejoin in their efforts to achieve the Republic, but alas that was not to be.

The days passed quickly with much excitement and speculation as news of an election was announced. The election, it was hoped, would put an end to the divisions that were at present threatening to tear the country apart by giving the people a voice. But many of the anti-Treaty troops were so determined to create a Republic that they felt that an election would be a waste of time.

It was a Collins and de Valera pact that had made the election possible. The IRA was suspicious of their motives, with many believing that Collins was merely playing for time by setting the election for the sixteenth of June, so that he had a chance to build up his relatively small Free State Army, should fighting break out.

Jack knew that most Republicans had not registered to vote in the past, as putting one's name on an electoral register gave the authorities your home address and with that, the names of your family members. Such information, in a time of war, could be used very effectively against the Republican movement, either by the British or by the Free State. Jack believed that the election would be a sham.

The lads were anxious. It was one thing to be in the thick of the fighting, with nothing more to think about other than keeping your head on your shoulders, but for most of the volunteers the current political stalemate was just too much to consider. Most volunteers left the political side of the movement to their leaders, whom they trusted unconditionally.

When you have a gun in your hand, Con Sullivan told Jack, you don't need a politician whispering in your ear. Jack was inclined to agree. The worst possible thing for a soldier was to have his mind on anything other than the job in hand. It was what got people killed. In an effort to block out the uncertainty of their collective future much of the time in the Courts was spent telling stories of their experiences during the Tan War, comparing scars and escapes, and singing. Con excelled in this regard and much was made of his rendition of Skibbereen, which usually brought a lively gathering down to quiet contemplation, reaffirming their belief in what they were doing. The song told the story of a dispossessed farmer who had to flee Ireland having been evicted from his farm by an English landlord.

O, son I loved my native land
With energy and pride,
'Till a blight came over all my crops,
My sheep and cattle died.
My rents and taxes were too high,
I could not them redeem.
And that's the cruel reason why I left old Skibbereen.

The garrison leaders became more accessible to the volunteers once the initial excitement of taking the courts had petered out. Jack, along with Jimmy and his cousin Terry, who had briefly turned up in the Courts, had all served in Fianna na hÉireann under the watchful eyes of Liam Mellows, and he remembered them well. Mellows had taught them basic military strategies—how to look after themselves in tough situations and how to fire and maintain a gun—things which had turned out to be extremely useful during the Tan fight when they spent weeks at a time on the run. And although Mellows and the rest of the commanders were usually busy, they made as much time for the men as possible, answering questions frankly when they could. There were some questions, however, that could not be answered.

Tension within the Four Courts was at an all-time high towards the end of May, with most volunteers getting nervous. They knew that something had to happen and they would have preferred it to happen sooner rather than later. The stress of waiting was beginning to tell on some volunteers and their unease grew with each day of occupation. Only the leadership of Mellows, O'Connor and O'Malley helped to keep the men at peace with one another.

They had spent their time fortifying the buildings in the Four Courts block, but it had proven a difficult task. Apart from the fact that the block was broken up into several free-standing buildings without adequate cover between them, the entire area was surrounded by high buildings that could provide excellent positions for enemy snipers. This would make communication within the Courts very difficult indeed if shooting actually began. And while sandbags and mines were used to their best advantage all around the buildings, Jack still felt that their positions were wide open to attack.

Once the main fortification work had been done, there was little to do other than wait for further orders. The time had begun to drag and nerves were fraying as the tension began to mount.

Jack sat back against a bookcase in the Law Library flicking through a huge tome on Common Law which was, it appeared, based on laws established by King John back in 1210. As he was just getting to the laws on property ownership, which he had never truly agreed with, Jimmy approached from where he had been sitting, watching Dublin pass by in the occasional sunlight that bathed the opposite quay.

'What do you make of the election?' Jimmy asked.

Jack closed the law book and looked up at his friend with sorrowful eyes. 'I don't think it will make a damned bit of a difference, Jimmy, and that's the truth,' Jack said, lowering his eyes to stare at his pistol, which lay on the floor beside him. Picking it up, he held it out in front of himself. 'This is the only thing that'll change anything. We're in a difficult position. If Collins and the Free Staters don't come after us, and I've a feeling they will once they have enough support, then the Brits will be back. To tell you the truth I don't like the way our leadership has set us up. It's as if they're looking for another blood sacrifice, another 1916. What were they thinking about when they chose which buildings to take? I mean look at us—Kilmainham Gaol, a good mile down the quays, the Four Courts, wide open and sitting on its own and then over to the far side of O'Connell Street, with no connection between the garrisons. What in the name of God were they thinking? If we're attacked we will be surrounded in no time and cut off from the rest of the army. And with the number of recruitment posters that the Free Staters are putting up, I'd be very surprised if they didn't outnumber us two-to-one already.' Jack looked back down at the law book on his lap. 'This is the kind of shit we have to put up with,' he said, bringing his fist down hard on the old book. 'The laws of another country, forced upon us. And now our own kind are turning on us and using the enemy's laws against us. They're calling us Irregulars for Christ sake. Irregulars! What right have they to subvert the Republic, to threaten us, the men who fought alongside them for the last few years, to tell us that we should toe the line and accept what we are given by the British. It's tearing me apart, Jimmy—that's how I feel about it,' Jack concluded, aware that his outburst was heard by all of the other volunteers present. It felt good to get it off his chest at last, having had the thoughts battling through his weary brain for the last four weeks of the courthouse occupation. The only respite he had had was the occasional raid or supply run that they had been asked to make. Otherwise, he had felt that it was like sitting in a prison cell waiting for the hangman to call out his name.

Jimmy was shocked at the outburst. Jack had always been a self-contained sort of fellow, reliable, strong and able to handle pressure. This wasn't the Jack he had seen during the Tan War, hurling petrol bombs into British Army tenders, setting the Black and Tans alight and picking them off with his rifle. Nor was it the Jack who had risked his own life to save a fellow volunteer who had fallen in the street from a bullet wound to the leg in a shootout. Jimmy could understand why Jack was feeling the way he was, but most volunteers just kept their thoughts to themselves and got on with it. Jack had been no exception in previous situations. Jimmy was worried about his friend. Sitting down on the floor beside him, Jimmy took Jack's pistol and rubbed it against his jacket until the blue-black metal shone deeply.

'Jaysus, that's a great pistol you've got there,' Jimmy said, taking out the magazine clip and then pushing it home again.

'You did ask,' Jack said, almost laughing.

'Aye, I did!' Jimmy said with a smile. 'I think most of us feel the same, but don't have the guts to say it. I've never seen you question the leadership like that before, Jack. Do you really think that they'd set us up to be slaughtered, to shed more blood for the Republic? I see men who want to live, who want to change the country. Look at Brugha—he's a man of the people—so are some of the others. They want to do the best for Ireland, to get the best out of the situation. You must trust them, Jack,' Jimmy said. 'If you can't trust them, who can you trust?'

'It's not that I don't trust them—I do, with all of my

heart. I'm just unsure about their method that's all. Remember how Liam taught us basic military strategy when we were in the Fianna? How stationary warfare is all well and good if you have the men and the equipment? How guerrilla warfare was the chosen form of war of the IRA because we didn't have the same sort of equipment and support behind us as the Brits? Well what are they playing at? The Brits have been replaced by something much worse—Irish Brits. They know who we are, how we think and they now have what the Brits used against us so well for centuries—the power of life and death. And all we can do is sit here and wait for them to come knocking on that big fucking door out there with their guns and bombs. We're like sitting ducks, God damn it!' Jack said, thinking that he was just scratching the surface of what he truly felt. There was a well of deep resentment and anger within him that was almost ready to explode.

Liam Mellows was in the room and had heard what Jack had been saying. He waited until Jack had finished and then came over, a look of concern on his face.

'Jack, what's bothering you?' Mellows asked.

'It just doesn't seem to make much sense, Liam. Taking the buildings we have goes against everything you taught us. We're not strong enough to hold Dublin on our own. And with the election set for the sixteenth, I just don't see us having much of a chance they way things are—they're recruiting men into the ranks of the Free State Army all the time,' Jack said, reiterating what he had said to Jimmy.

'Look, Jack, we've been through these arguments at Executive level for a few weeks now and this was the way we chose to go. You see it's a political as well as a military battle we're fighting here. We have to let the people see that the Republic is safe in our hands and to do that we have to maintain a position of power in the city. We need to control it. And the best expression of control we can make is by holding the nerve centre of the system. Without the courts, any form of democracy is impossible. Holding the Four Courts is also a symbolic gesture that lets the people see that we are serious, that we're not just the renegades that the Free Staters and the papers are claiming. You see, going back to guerrilla warfare, while it would be the best thing to do from a military standpoint, and that's how most of us think, politically it would be the death knell. We would be painted as the soldiers who didn't want to stop fighting—not for political reasons, but for other, less noble reasons. It would turn public opinion against us immediately. That's why we've taken the buildings we have,' Mellows said, placing his hand on Jack's shoulder and tightening his grip.

Jack looked down at the floor, reasoning the argument that Mellows had just put forward.

'Look, I understand what you mean about having to keep the people on our side but why couldn't we have taken over a portion of the city? Say, the whole of O'Connell Street, or even a section from the Four Courts that stretched over to O'Connell Street if the Courts are that important. It just feels like we've exposed ourselves unnecessarily, that we could be surrounded and taken within a few days. I don't want this to turn into another blood sacrifice and I know some of the leaders think that way. I've heard them speak about it. I want to fight; I want to see a free and united Ireland. It's in my blood, my heart. But by Christ I want to live, too. My father gave his life in 1916—do we have to do the same? Can we not even have a decent chance of winning this time? I was taught by my father, and by you, Liam, that we could win if we never gave up. We have right on our side. Every book and pamphlet I've read tells me so. We have to keep fighting until we get what we want, but the fight has to be a fair fight. It can't be another blood sacrifice! How many more men have to die before the leaders see that?' Jack said, pain obvious in all of his words.

'I know you're right in what you're saying, Jack. I feel the same, as you know. But the Executive ruled this way and there's nothing to be done about it. You are either with the Executive or against us. And I think you're with us, Jack. I know you are,' Mellows said, looking Jack in the eye.

'Come on, Jack,' Jimmy said, 'sure don't you have the rest of us here. We've been fighting together for years now and we've never let each other down. What makes you think that we will now? Besides, I can't see Collins sending his men against us.'

'What do you think, Liam? Do you think that Collins will send his men out against us?' Jack asked.

'I think he might. Either way we've got to be prepared. Don't underestimate the IRA, Jack, most of the southern divisions are against the Treaty, and practically all the Dublin Brigade is too. The same applies to Mayo, Sligo and Tipperary. We have thousands of men behind us. It's not the same as it was in 1916. This time they're ready to fight because the time is right and the prize of a Republic is there for the taking. Just one more push, you know,' Mellows said, shaking Jack gently by the arm in an effort to drive home his point. Mellows was a small man but he was strong—both intellectually and physically.

'So what happens if the Courts fall? Do we surrender? Do we fight to the last man?' Jimmy asked. 'What's the plan?'

'We have an escape route planned. Don't worry. There's a sewer system that runs from here that'll take us out of the building and get us far enough away to escape, if it comes to that. That's one of the many reasons the Four

Courts were chosen. We've done our homework on this, lads, trust us,' Mellows, said with a smile. 'We know what we're doing.'

Mellows walked away, hoping that he had answered some of Jack's questions, but Jack sat there, still unconvinced, flicking through the law book he had on his lap.

Barry Murphy approached from one of the courtrooms and greeted Jack and Jimmy.

'All right? What are you two up to?' Barry inquired.

'Not much,' Jimmy replied. 'Jack's been asking questions.'

'What do you mean?' Barry asked.

'Ah, he means nothing, Barry, he means nothing. What have you been doing?' Jack asked.

'We were reorganising the ammunition downstairs and doing a little stocktaking,' Barry said.

'So, how long could we hold out?' Jimmy asked, joking.

'About three days under heavy fire,' Barry said, without a hint of humour.

'Three days?' Jimmy repeated.

'Are they planning to do some more raids for ammo?' Jack asked.

'I don't know—there's been some talk of a Civic Guards barracks in Kildare, but I haven't heard anything other than that.'

'I'm not surprised,' Jack said, growing increasingly unhappy at the state of things.

Chapter Six

As details of the Collins-de Valera election pact became fully known some Republicans began to see a light at the end of the tunnel. The pact was proposing a panel of candidates from both pro- and anti-Treaty Sinn Féin. The plan was for those elected to form a coalition government. It seemed to be a logical step forward. It was at least a step in the right direction, as Jimmy had said to Jack. Apart from a coalition between the opposing parties, the pact allowed for an Army Council of eight members, with four members coming from either side of the Republican divide. This, it was hoped, would reunite the IRA and put a stop to the recent slide towards all-out civil war. But most Republicans were still not convinced.

In Jack's eyes the election and the pact, which de Valera had made without extensive consultation with the Army Executive, were merely delaying tactics. He believed that the Free State Army would swell both its ranks and public support as the Dáil attempted to put an end to the seeming anarchy that was sweeping the country. Jack knew that support for the anti-Treaty IRA was dwindling somewhat in the onslaught of media coverage that labeled them 'Irregulars'. Only months before, the same newspapers were heralding the IRA as Ireland's saviours. And before that again they referred to them as scoundrels and rebels. It seemed that the editorial line was drawn in constantly shifting sands and at present the sands appeared to be shifting in Collins' favour.

A big bone of contention with most anti-Treaty volunteers was the idea of a British-dictated constitution. Collins planned to publish the constitution ten days before the election so as to give the people a chance to make up their minds as to how they should vote. As it turned out, however, Collins didn't get the constitution he so badly desired. Despite several trips to London in a bid to negotiate the wording, Collins returned with a document that still contained the Oath of Allegiance—something that no anti-Treaty Republican could possibly accept.

Jack attempted to explain to Jimmy how the proposed electoral pact would work.

'The Free Staters are looking to get some of our leaders into the government as external ministers. If Brugha, Stack and Childers are elected they can be a part of the government, only without having to pledge an oath of allegiance to the Crown,' Jack explained.

'But Collins still hasn't released the new version of the constitution he's going to put forward,' Jimmy said.

'Aye, and that means he hasn't got what he wanted from Lloyd George. The constitution game he's playing is a ruse. He's just biding his time; he's stealing our votes by claiming that he's one of us at heart. I don't trust him,' Jack said as Con entered the room.

'Collins has just back-tracked on the pact,' Con said, having heard the news from another volunteer. All of the volunteers present shook their heads in disbelief.

'That's it then,' Jack said slowly. 'He's looking for war. He's left us no way out.'

Polling day passed off relatively peacefully and was followed two days later by an arms raid on the Civic Guard barracks in Kildare town by members of the Four Courts garrison. A large quantity of arms and ammunition was seized in the raid without loss of life, along with a truck and an armoured car, which the garrison nicknamed 'The Mutineer'. It was parked outside the front gates of the Courts on their return with a complement of volunteers manning the machine guns.

The following day an IRA Convention was scheduled to take place in the Mansion House on Dawson Street where representatives from all over the country could have their say. Jack and Jimmy were asked to accompany Liam Mellows and Rory O'Connor's Four Courts' delegation. All were anxious to find out which way the Executive might go as the country awaited the results of the election.

Jack and Jimmy followed Mellows and O'Connor at close quarters along with a guard of around fifteen other volunteers, who were ordered to take up a position outside the Mansion House whilst the Convention got under way. Jack and Jimmy were brought inside and took their seats near the podium.

While many members of the Executive, under Liam Lynch's guidance, had taken a pro-negotiation stance in relation to the acting government, the Four Courts garrison, headed by Rory O'Connor and Liam Mellows disagreed strongly. They could no longer see the point of conducting negotiations with a government that had gone back on the election pact and that had thrust an unacceptable constitution upon them. Jack was inclined to agree.

When the well-known Cork Republican Tom Barry began to speak he brought the issue down to one simple motion: to give the British an ultimatum to leave the country in seventy-two hours or face war. A show of hands seemed to carry the motion but, under pressure, a ballot was taken. The motion was defeated. The anti-Treaty IRA was now firmly split down the middle, with

O'Connor and Mellows walking out of the meeting and heading back to the Four Courts. As a result of the split Liam Lynch and his men returned to Cork, reducing the Four Courts garrison somewhat and increasing their sense of isolation.

Jack could no longer contain himself as they marched back to the Four Courts. Ignoring Jimmy's pleas to keep his mouth shut, Jack strode ahead to O'Connor and Mellows and interrupted their conversation.

'Can't this wait, Jack?' Mellows asked, knowing that he and O'Connor had a lot of serious talking to do.

'Sorry, Liam, but no, it can't,' Jack replied.

'Well, what is it?' O'Connor asked.

'I agree with your stand on negotiating with the government—they proved that they can't be trusted, but I was wondering where that leaves us. The motion that Tom Barry proposed has more or less split the IRA in two when what we need most is unification, a common strategy...'

'I agree with you, Jack,' O'Connor replied. 'What we need is strength and unity, but we won't get that dealing with Lynch and Brugha, who still seem to believe that Collins will do an about-face and rejoin the struggle for the Republic. We all know that is never going to happen. I've taken the stand I have in the hope of reuniting the IRA so that Collins can see that there's no way forward without our participation. And if he does decide to move against us then what will Lynch and Brugha do? Sit back and wait for a negotiated settlement? I don't think that will happen.'

'So you think that by walking out of the Convention you just might reunite the IRA?' Jack asked, unsurely.

'If Collins does Lloyd George's dirty work for him, I've no doubt in my mind that the rift we saw develop today will heal, and heal very quickly indeed,' O'Connor said.

'So in the meantime we sit tight in the Four Courts and wait for Collins to attack?' Jack asked.

'It's his move. Either he's with us or against us. Any fool can see that he has taken us for a long ride with this election and constitution game he's been playing. Well, we won't play along anymore,' O'Connor said.

'So what do you think Brugha and Lynch will do?' Jack asked.

'I think they'll wait and see how Collins treats us. That's the use of having a split—it's easier to see how the opposition is working, who they're working on, so to speak. If Collins starts offering more inducements to Lynch and Brugha whilst threatening us, they'll soon see what he has in mind,' O'Connor said with a ghost of a smile.

Jack had a feeling that the split had been well choreographed to achieve what O'Connor had just outlined. Everyone knew that there would be men present who would report back to Collins and the British government on the course that the convention had taken. The reports would merely bring events to a head sooner rather than later. If O'Connor's game worked, and it seemed likely, Collins would use the opportunity of the split to force an agreement on the weakened Four Courts garrison, or threaten them with attack. And when O'Connor and Mellows refused to deal with Collins or go along the road that the Treaty had laid down, Collins' hands would be tied. He would either bow to pressure from London and put an end to the Four Courts occupation, or he would see that an opportunity to rally their forces against the British still existed and that the Republic was still within reach without the ugly prospect of all-out civil war.

'Jack, wait before telling the other volunteers about this. We'll be holding a garrison meeting this evening where everything will be discussed. We know how the lads feel.

We're just trying to get everything right in case Collins or the British attack us. It's a game of wait and see at the moment. We need to ensure that we are in the best possible position. Don't forget that we are the ones who are pledged to uphold the Republic. We have right on our side. Whatever we do, it is for the good of the country, for the good of the people of Ireland, but you know that already, don't you?' Mellows said with a smile.

'I've always known that,' Jack replied, feeling an ever-growing bond between himself and Liam Mellows, whilst at the same time beginning to appreciate the strategy that he and O'Connor seemed to be working. Only time would tell.

When the delegation got back to the Four Courts word spread like wildfire of the split that had taken place between the leadership of the Executive as Lynch's men packed up and left. Disquiet and unease filled the beautiful old court buildings as volunteers voiced their fears and aspirations without knowing what would finally happen. It was as if their leaders had just launched them into limbo—a limbo that seemed to have but one exit: war. Whichever way the pendulum of time and politics would swing it would lead to an outbreak of hostilities. It was inevitable in the minds of most. Fear and uncertainty quickly replaced the boredom, which had become commonplace over the previous weeks. Even the bravest men among them were now filled with doubts, filled with fears of being abandoned when the bullets finally began to fly.

When Mellows and O'Connor announced a meeting for later that evening a palpable sense of relief filled the air.

Jack and Jimmy took up their usual positions in the east wing on the first floor overlooking Chancery Place and

Inns' Quay. At the window to their right stood volunteers Tom Wall and John Cusack, who had gone strangely silent upon hearing of the split. They were usually lively enough fellows, Jack thought, turning to Jimmy as he began to speak.

'What do you think they're playing at,' Jimmy asked. 'You spoke to them, what did they say?'

'It's a little complicated, Jimmy, but I think that the split was agreed before the convention took place. I could be wildly off the mark, but I got a funny feeling listening to O'Connor that he has a plan. Just like Collins has been playing with us over the election, I think the Executive is beginning to play with him and the government in the same way. I think the Executive are pretending a split has happened in order to bring Collins out of the sidelines, to get him to nail his colours to the mast. We've been hanging on a thread for the last month or so and I think the Executive believe this will force the issue with the Dáil. They have to decide which way they're going to go on the Treaty once and for all. Now that people have had a chance to read that thing that Collins was calling a constitution, I think they might change their minds and come back to our side,' Jack said, a look of deep thought etching furrows in his brow.

'So you think that they're just pretending there's a split to get Collins to make his move?'

'I think so,' Jack replied.

'But if Collins thinks that there's a split, surely he'll decide to come down harder on us, to force us round to his way of thinking....'

'But that's the whole plan, I think. If Collins starts playing heavy guns with us, then Lynch and Brugha will understand that he has no intention of changing his mind and working for an Irish Republic, so they'll be back with us and Collins will see that he has to move either way. The Executive is forcing the issue with him—they want the matter settled sooner rather than later. The propaganda in the papers and the Free State Army recruitment is damaging our support. We need to move soon before our support is completely gone,' Jack said, beginning to feel a little confused in his thoughts.

Jimmy shook his head. He didn't want to admit it, but he was lost. He could understand why an apparent split might make sense, but he wasn't sure about what it would ultimately achieve. Jack didn't really know either and it bothered him. It had all seemed so clear when he was speaking to O'Connor and Mellows on the way back from the Mansion House. Now, it seemed scrambled—a puzzle in many oddly shaped pieces that he couldn't quite put together. He knew he understood it deep down, in his heart, but his head was just not dealing with it. His moment of clarity had gone.

The meeting called to order by O'Connor, Mellows and O'Malley was not what the men were expecting and not what Jack had reasoned from his brief conversation with O'Connor. According to what O'Connor now told the amassed volunteers there was no turning back. The decisions made had put them on a pathway to war—of that there could be no mistake. O'Connor's words rose like fire as he whipped the young volunteers into a veritable frenzy of agreement. Jack felt himself being carried along by this tide of thought until it was the only thing that filled his mind.

'We have to make a stand against what the Dáil is forcing upon us. Without that stand people will say that we let the dream of the Republic die when it could still be a reality. We must stand firm at this hour of desperation. We must show the world that we will not accept the whim of the British, or subjugation by their lackeys in the Dáil. You may feel afraid and uncertain at what will happen and that is only natural—but when the time comes the true soldiers of the Irish Republic will stand shoulder to shoulder and our true comrades will join us in our fight for Irish freedom. Have no fear of that, lads,' O'Connor finished, seeing that his work was done and that the men were fully behind him.

All thoughts of clandestine deals and splits had vanished from the minds of both Jack and Jimmy, leaving nothing more than the ideal of freedom, the glory of fighting the fight, the importance of being strong, proud and courageous. That was what mattered now. The world was watching them and they could, if O'Connor was right, set the country on the road to a Republic after all—if only they held firm their principles and kept the faith.

Once the meeting had ended, Mellows made his way over to where Jack and Jimmy were standing.

'Well, what do you think?' Mellows asked.

'I think you're right. We do need to show the world what we've been fighting for, what we will die for, if necessary,' Jack said.

'You seemed a little uncertain about our methods earlier, Jack,' Mellows said, wondering what it was that had so quickly changed his mind.

'I had some strange idea that we were being put forward as sacrificial lambs, but I see now that if we are to be anything it's a catalyst.'

'That's what we are depending on, Jack. And you, Jimmy?'

'I agree with Jack and I trust the Executive. Once we stand firm then no one can deny us our right to be heard.'

Mellows smiled warmly.

'If only all the other volunteers were as focused as you

two we'd have the Republic in no time at all.'

'What's happening this year about Bodenstown?' Jack asked, referring to the annual Republican pilgrimage to the grave of Theobald Wolfe Tone in County Wicklow where leaders of the movement gave speeches from the graveside on the future of the movement.

'We'll be going along as usual,' Mellows said. 'But we'll have to make sure that there are enough men here to hold the buildings in case anyone tries to attack.'

'Right you are,' Jimmy said.

'But I suppose you two would like to come down?' Mellows said, knowing full well that that was what Jack had in mind when he brought the subject up.

'Well, if you think it would be all right we'd really like to go,' Jack said.

'Well, we'll need a few guns in the car, I suppose,' Mellows said with a smile. 'You can come down with myself and Rory.'

The summer sunshine was almost blinding on the drive down to Bodenstown in County Kildare. Jimmy was driving and Jack was seated beside him with a couple of loaded revolvers and a rifle on his lap. O'Connor and Mellows sat in the rear.

The open-topped touring car swept along the narrow country lanes, the wind blowing through the hair of its occupants, providing a relief that none of the men had had since they took over the Four Courts. Mellows and O'Connor were in a sombre mood given the recent split in the IRA, but even they managed to find a smile as the beautiful countryside made its impression on them. The rolling hills and green pastures, the cows and horses on the land, had a calming effect on the four men. Surely there can be no better way to spend a summer's day, Jack thought, seeing rabbits scurry from the road into the relative sanctuary of the hedge.

Mellows was going over a speech he had written for the commemoration and O'Connor was giving him some ideas as he worked his way through it, scribbling out passages and re-writing where necessary. The Wolfe Tone speeches were always something to look forward to in the Republican calendar of events. And this year would be more interesting than most, given the state of the country and the state of the IRA. Leaders from all over the country would be waiting to hear what O'Connor and Mellows had to say of their continued actions in the face of the recent split. It was a chance to put across their side of the argument—something that was not always possible at a convention. The opportunity was also present to reaffirm one's belief in the Republican ideal while paying respect to the father of Irish Republicanism, Theobald Wolfe Tone.

'This should be interesting,' Jimmy said, afraid to take his eyes off the road, lest the long car find its way into a ditch.

'I hope it goes well. This could be the only chance we get to make our case to the rest of the movement,' Jack said, Mellows lifting his head from his papers as he did so.

'Don't worry, Jack,' Mellows said. 'It occasionally takes longer for some people to see the truth. All we need to do is to show them the way forward and they will follow. In their hearts they know we're right, but they are hoping that the Free Staters will change their position to accommodate them. That won't happen. As soon as the rest of the army sees that they'll be back with us.'

'I hope you're right,' Jack said, looking Mellows in the eye.

He had never seen such confident idealism in his life. Mellows positively radiated it. It was an all-consuming and overpowering aura of strength, conviction and humanity.

He's a born leader and one of the best minds that the movement has, Jack thought, as he saw the pain in those powerful eyes. It seemed as though he was being pulled apart by the nature of the circumstances in which he found himself. Damned if you do and damned if you don't. He knew there could be no winners if it came to civil war, but he also believed that his fight was for a just cause that could not be allowed to wane for personal or selfish reasons. This was why Jack admired him so much.

'Of course he's right,' O'Connor said, breaking the curious spell that existed briefly between Jack and Mellows. 'The rest of the movement will see that there is no way forward in their dealings with the Provisional Government. They'll see that Collins and Griffith have sold us out and are merely trying to break us down, split us up, so they have the upper hand. We've made the right moral choice and given time the rest of the army will see that,' O'Connor said, satisfied with his beliefs.

Jimmy slowed the car down as he rounded a bend in the road.

'Roadblock,' he said.

'Us or them?' Mellows asked.

'Staters,' Jack replied. 'I can see the uniforms.'

'Well, we're not going to turn around and run. Have your guns at the ready, lads. Let's see what they want,' O'Connor said.

Jimmy drove up to the roadblock slowly. It consisted of four men one Lancia armoured car and three milk churns, which they had used to block the road.

'What's all the fuss?' Mellows asked as a Stater approached the car.

'Who are ye and where are ye heading?' the man asked.

He was a big country man and he didn't seem very intelligent, Jack thought to himself on hearing his accent.

'We're with Collins' staff. We're going to the Wolfe Tone Memorial,' Mellows said sharply. 'Now get those bloody churns off the road or your commanding officer will hear all about this,' he finished.

'Sorry, sir. We were told to keep an eye out for Irregulars,' he said, looking away.

He looked slightly embarrassed as he instructed his men to move the roadblock. Jack stifled a laugh as Jimmy nudged him in the ribs.

'Carry on,' O'Connor said to the men as Jimmy drove through the roadblock. All four men laughed loudly as the car sped along the road.

'That's one for the grandchildren,' Mellows said with a smile. They all laughed again.

The men were silent for the rest of the journey to Bodenstown, feeling the importance of the task in hand. If O'Connor and Mellows could persuade Brugha and Lynch's men to come back over to their side, if they could somehow show them that the Collins plan was to split them up, to defeat them from within, they might once again have unity amongst the anti-Treaty units of the IRA.

Upon arrival at the cemetery, O'Connor and Mellows were met by groups of men at the gates. Jack and Jimmy stood behind Mellows and O'Connor, their revolvers under their coats. The atmosphere was electric and the divisions felt within the movement were glaringly obvious, as the different factions took up their positions near the grave of Wolfe Tone. The summer sun warmed the crowd as a pipe and flute band began to play.

Jack had never seen so many familiar faces at the commemoration. Every leader he had heard of since joining the movement was there. Brugha, Lynch, Stack, and the rest of them stood around quietly chatting, making pledges of loyalty and re-affirming their beliefs in each other's views and intentions.

'This,' Jack told Jimmy, 'is where we'll either win or lose. It's all going to happen here today.' Jimmy nodded, his eyes scanning the crowds, his hand firmly on the wooden grip of his Webley revolver.

Once the band had finished playing their medley, the speeches began in earnest, with some of the older and more respected Republicans taking their turn to celebrate Wolfe Tone's ideals. But the crowd was growing agitated as the time ticked on. The majority was there to hear what Mellows and O'Connor would say of their recent decision to walk out of the convention in the Mansion House. They didn't have to wait long.

Mellows took his place in front of the grave and began to speak. His voice carried on the light summer winds to the edges of the crowd that had moved a little closer to hear. There was a fire in his belly as he began his short speech, calling for a concerted effort and a redoubling of commitment from the leaders of the IRA. Mellows' words rang in Jack's ears. He reminded the crowd of the Proclamation of Independence and how it was the duty of every Republican to see the fight through to the bitter end. The Treaty, he said, would cause divisions in Irish society for generations if it were allowed to persist. He asked that Republicans re-examine their commitment to the movement and its central ideals and reminded them that a Republic was still within their grasp if they were brave enough to hold on.

Applause filled the graveyard as Mellows stepped down. Jack and Jimmy stood close to O'Connor, who had been talking with IRA leaders from all over the country since his arrival, renewing acquaintances, forming alliances and making pacts. Mellows came over and joined the fray as a southern commander questioned O'Connor's view of the present situation and how the outcome of the election might change matters entirely. It had been five days since the election and the results were still not in, leaving Republican and non-Republican alike in a sort of political limbo from which they could not escape until the votes had been counted in full. O'Connor argued that the results of the election would mean nothing given Collins' repudiation of the de Valera pact and the nature of the constitution he had thrust upon the people of Ireland. There was much agreement. The day ended with pledges of support from undecided commanders in the event of an outbreak of hostilities. That gave them something of a breathing space, Jack thought—a chance to stand and fight if that was what it would come down to. Everything was still so uncertain.

Chapter Seven

O'Connor gathered the Four Courts' garrison together for an impromptu meeting. Sir Henry Wilson, a British Field Marshal, was shot dead outside his London home, apparently by two IRA men. Lloyd George had given Wilson carte blanche in his use of force against northern Catholics, and he was despised as a result. O'Connor didn't say if the Executive was behind the killing, but the general feeling was that it was. The killing had enraged the British Government to the point where O'Connor thought that they might attack the Four Courts in an act of retaliation. Such a move, it was believed, could reunite the IRA overnight, both pro- and anti-Treaty units. But the British did not attack and the next few days were very tense indeed.

Given that the split had still not righted itself and that they were, for the present at least, alone in their actions, it was more important than ever to ensure that their comrades in the North were being fed a good supply of weapons, transport and food, O'Connor said. That meant more raids for these items would have to take place.

'I want five volunteers to form a raiding party with Commandant Henderson. We'll be raiding for petrol and enforcing the Belfast boycott on one or two Dublin businesses that haven't been paying attention,' O'Connor said, Henderson standing beside him.

The Belfast boycott was an attempt by the Republican leadership to place a stranglehold on all businesses in

Dublin that were continuing to do business with pro-British parties in Belfast. It was hoped that, by threatening companies in Dublin, commerce in Belfast would suffer as a result. Collins had tried to put a stop to the boycott under pressure from the British government, but the Republican leadership continued to enforce it nonetheless.

Five men stepped forward—all of them from Henderson's own area. It seemed strange sometimes, Jack thought, the way officers occasionally asked for volunteers instead of giving direct orders. It was better to let the men decide what actions they were to be involved in. If there was going to be shooting, then it would be better to have men who had volunteered and not some reticent young fellows itching to get back to the relative safety of the Four Courts.

Once the short meeting came to an end everyone was sent back to his respective posts—some with the newer Mauser carbine rifles which had mysteriously appeared in the last few days. The volunteers had been asking where they had come from, but no one seemed to know. The only thing they knew for sure was that officers from the staff were making journeys abroad in search of arms and support.

Amongst them was Sean McBride, the Assistant Director of Operations, while Mellows, the Quartermaster, was also making attempts to import arms for the fight that would almost inevitably come.

Jack stood at his post overlooking Chancery Place and Inns' Quay, Jimmy beside him, cleaning his rifle.

'Things seemed to have stepped up a gear, don't they?' Jack said.

'They've turned the Records Office into a munitions factory. They've got some engineers down there building grenades and messing about with bombs,' Jimmy said.

'Well, I'm sure we'll hear it if they make a mess of it,' Jack said with a smile.

'You can be damned well sure of that,' Tom Wall said from the next window to the right.

'I've been down there,' Cusack said, shaking his head.

'What are they doing exactly?' Jack asked.

'They're casting grenade shells from hot metal and filling them with explosives and detonators—it's amazing what these blokes can do,' he said, returning his gaze to the far side of the river, where two women could be seen waving handkerchiefs in the direction of the courts. 'Looks like someone's ladies are saying hello.'

Jack and Jimmy glanced over to where Cusack was looking and saw two young women.

'Is that Kathy and Helen?' Jimmy remarked trying to get a better look.

'I'm not sure, I can't make them out,' Jack said squinting somewhat in the process.

'Doesn't Ernie O'Malley have a good set of field glasses? Maybe you could ask him if you could borrow them?' Tom Wall suggested.

'I'll see if I can get them,' Jimmy said, 'where is he?'

'I think he's downstairs in the round room,' Cusack said looking out across the river.

Five minutes later Jimmy returned with O'Malley's field glasses and approached the window, holding them up to his eyes. Jack grabbed them playfully.

'She's my girl, not yours—if anybody's going to look at her it's me,' Jack said with a grin, nudging Jimmy in the ribs. 'You've got those lovely Cumann na mBan girls to drool over.'

Jack raised the field glasses to his eyes and brought the lenses into focus on the figures across the river. They were Kathy and Helen.

'Jaysus, it is them,' Jack said.

'Maybe you should have a word with Seán and see if you can go over to meet them for a few minutes,' Jimmy suggested. Jack nodded, handed the glasses back to Jimmy and headed for the stairs. Jimmy raised the glasses to his eyes and had a look for himself.

In the round room Seán Fitzgerald and Ernie O'Malley were talking quietly as Jack approached.

'How are you Jack?' Seán asked. 'You've met Ernie O'Malley before, haven't you?'

'Yes, sir, I have,' Jack replied, not wanting to appear too casual around an officer he didn't know very well.

'So, what can I do for you?' Seán asked, seeing that Jack was moving somewhat impatiently from foot to foot.

'Well, it seems my girl is outside, across the river, and I was wondering if I could go out for a few minutes, just to tell her to go home, like, you know,' Jack said, almost believing himself.

'Kathy, is it?' Seán inquired.

'Yes sir, Kathy.'

'Fair enough, but take Jimmy or someone along with you just in case there is any trouble,' Seán said with a smile. 'And tell her I was asking for her.'

'Thanks, Seán,' Jack said before going off in search of Barry, his sister's boyfriend.

Jack found Barry playing cards on the third floor with some volunteers from Clanbrassil Street. He looked up when he saw Jack approaching.

'All right?' Barry asked.

'Helen and Kathy are across the river and Seán has given us permission to go over. Do you want to come?' Jack asked, knowing the answer would be yes.

Barry smiled warmly, dropped his cards and got up.

'Sorry lads, duty calls,' he said with a smile, heading out

of the room with Jack.

Kathy stood by the river wall. She had a brown paper parcel tied with string in her arms. A look of relief swept her face as she saw Jack and Barry approach. The two girls rushed over to greet their young men with hugs and kisses. It was the first time they had seen each other in over four weeks.

'Oh, Jack!' Kathy sighed as she held Jack tightly.

'I've missed you,' Jack whispered, squeezing her with all of his might.

'Are you well? Are you eating?' Kathy inquired, looking into Jack's eyes. He looked a little tired, a little run-down, Kathy thought.

'I'm fine, darling. We all are. It's so good to see you again,' Jack said.

'We've been trying to get over here for the past week, but the Free Staters stopped us getting through until today.'

'It's getting dangerous. You shouldn't be here. We're expecting trouble to break out any day. It's just a matter of time, you know.'

'Would you rather I didn't come?' Kathy asked with a smile. She knew he was always happy to see her, whatever the circumstances were.

'Don't be silly; of course I am! I'm just worried about you, that's all,' Jack admitted.

'You shouldn't worry, Jack, not now. Helen and I have joined Cumann na mBan,' she said proudly.

'You've done what?' Jack asked, wondering if his hearing was failing him.

'We joined Cumann na mBan last week. We're being trained as field nurses.'

'Why didn't you talk to me first?' Jack asked, annoyed at not being consulted.

'I do have a mind of my own, you know!' Kathy said, a little irritated by his attitude.

'And what did your parents have to say about this?'

'My Ma says she's proud of me, but my Da wasn't too keen at the notion of it,' Kathy replied.

Jack took a step back and looked at Kathy. He thought for a moment of all the times she had been worried about him, how she had stood by him throughout the War of Independence and the Tan War. She had done everything she could during those dark days to help him. She had been his rock, his base, and his reason to continue. He suddenly felt guilty about what he had said. 'I'm sorry, darling, I'm proud of you too, but it could be dangerous. I never thought you would go and do something like that!'

'Well, someone has to look after you lot,' she said jokingly, a smile breaking as she spoke. She knew he had come around, and that he was just concerned for her wellbeing.

'I can't stay too long,' Jack said, looking over his shoulder at the courts. 'I told Seán that I'd only be a few minutes.'

'I've brought you a parcel of food and clothes and a small bottle of Jameson,' Kathy said handing it to Jack. Helen brought one for Barry, too.'

Jack smiled lovingly and reached out to caress her face. 'I'm sorry we haven't been able to get away these past weeks. Everything has just been so unsure.'

'Don't worry, I understand. It'll all be finished with when Collins sees what a mess he's created.'

'I hope you're right, but it doesn't look like that just now.'

'Well, if the fighting starts you can be sure we'll be there,' Kathy said, looking over towards Helen and then back into Jack's eyes, 'patching you lot up.'

Jack wondered if it was possible to love anyone as much as he loved Kathy. She was so beautiful, so caring and so wonderful that he felt he didn't quite deserve her.

'Where are you being trained?' Jack asked.

'Over in Suffolk Street. They have us typing letters to be sent to foreign governments when they're not teaching us how to dress wounds.'

'Where will you be stationed?'

'I don't know just yet, but I'll ask if I can come to the Four Courts when I finish my training next week.'

'We'd best be getting back,' Barry said to Jack as he hugged Helen tightly.

'Aye, let's get going,' Jack said, kissing Kathy firmly on the lips. 'I'll see you soon, darling, and take care. I'll be thinking about you.'

'You too,' Kathy said, tears welling in her eyes as Jack and Barry crossed the bridge, parcels under their arms. Sometimes, she thought, it was as though God was playing with them, that he was testing them.

Later that evening two of the six-man raiding and boy-cott enforcement party returned to the courts with some bad news. As they had been collecting petrol for the northbound trucks that would deliver supplies to the IRA in Ulster they had been jumped by a Free State patrol. Commandant Leo Henderson had been arrested. The volunteers, who were greatly outnumbered, had made a run for it. So far only two had returned to the courts. Mellows and O'Connor were furious and set about planning a reprisal arrest which they might use as leverage to get Henderson back, whilst showing the Provisional Government that they meant business. Following a lengthy staff meeting held to decide who they might take hostage, a decision was reached. Collins and Mulcahy were suggested as possible targets by Ernie O'Malley along with Ginger O'Connell—the Assistant Chief of Staff of the Free State Army. In the end it was decided to go for O'Connell, whose whereabouts was known and whose abduction might prove a little easier than that of Collins.

O'Malley asked Jimmy if he would like to take part in the reprisal arrest and if he could suggest another two volunteers. Jimmy smiled confidently and said he would go along, whilst taking a sideways glance at Jack, who nodded sharply.

'Jack Larkin here is a good man, sir,' Jimmy said without hesitation.

'Would you like to come along, Jack?' O'Malley asked.

'Yes sir,' Jack replied.

'And we have another man in our unit who would love to get out of the courts for a few hours, Con Sullivan, sir. He's on the next floor with the Clanbrassil Street unit,' Jimmy said.

'Very well, see if he wants to come along. We'll need to be well armed in case we meet any opposition,' O'Malley said. 'We're arresting Ginger O'Connell.'

'Ginger O'Connell?' Jimmy repeated, slightly taken aback. 'Where will we find him?'

'We know where he'll be. Right, get everything together and meet me downstairs in half an hour,' O'Malley said, turning to leave.

The four men soon found themselves driving across the city and over the Grand Canal. They stopped on the far side of the canal just up the road from the house where O'Malley said O'Connell was to be found.

'O'Connell may have some people with him so we're

going to wait until he leaves the house on his own. If we storm the house we might get more than we bargained for,' O'Malley said.

An hour passed with people coming and going from the house before O'Connell left and headed on foot towards the canal. On O'Malley's orders Jimmy pulled the car up alongside O'Connell and O'Malley got out, Con behind him with a revolver in his hand. A quick tap on O'Connell's shoulder and the game was up. O'Malley explained what they were doing, disarmed him, and placed him in the back of the car, Con on one side, Jack on the other.

'What on earth do you think you're going to achieve by kidnapping me?' O'Connell asked.

'Your men took Leo Henderson earlier today, so we're taking you. When he's released, you'll be released,' O'Malley said, as Jimmy headed back down towards the river via Westmoreland Street.

'I hope they blow the hell out of you lot in the courts!' O'Connell replied.

As the traffic slowed O'Connell tried to make a run for it but was quickly stopped by Con, who, on O'Malley's orders, put him on the floor of the car and sat on him. Jack smiled to himself as he held his revolver on the man. Only a few weeks ago it would have been the last thing in the world that he thought he would be doing, yet here he was.

Once back in the relative safety of the courts, with O'Connell in the guardroom, Jack, Jimmy and Con returned to their posts to hear that the election results had been finally announced. The result was what most Republicans had expected. Fifty-eight pro-Treaty politicians were elected compared with only thirty-five anti-Treaty representatives out of a total of one hundred and thirty-eight seats. The remaining seats went to the Labour

Party, the Farmers' Party, independents and the Unionist Party. The country was edging closer to war by the day.

Two days later, at around nine in the evening, the first rumours of a likely attack filtered down the ranks to the volunteers. According to Barry a friar had heard of the attack through his sources and the word had been passed on. Shortly afterwards the officers began to assign tasks to the various units within the courts.

Jack and Jimmy were sent out with orders to dig trenches inside the main gates. It was hoped that the trenches would slow up or stop any advancing armoured cars that might attempt to gain entrance to the grounds. Other units were sent out to mine the approach roads. As they did, however, Free State armoured cars arrived, the occupants got out and began to cut the wires to the batteries that were set to detonate the mines. The men found it very frustrating. But, having been given orders not to open fire, they restrained themselves.

Jack and Jimmy were working up a sweat with their pick-axes as they dislodged the huge paving stones that ran inside the perimeter fence of the courts, to prepare the ground for trenches.

'Those bastards,' Jack said, as he saw the first armoured car pull up and its occupants begin to work on disarming the mines that had been laid. 'I don't understand. We've been told that they're planning to attack us—their own former comrades—and our leaders won't even allow us to defend ourselves.'

'I think they're playing a little game called 'who fires first',' Jimmy said raising his eyebrows. 'And we have to wait and let them do the firing.'

'It doesn't make any sense,' Jack said, beginning to dig.

'All we're doing is letting them get closer and closer to see what we're doing. They'll be able to take this place in a day if we don't tighten up our security.'

'You're not wrong. But Mellows and McKelvey are getting the lads to put up barbed wire barricades all over the place,' Jimmy said, wiping the sweat from his brow.

It was heavy work. They hadn't done much in the way of physical work for well over a month. The last heavy lifting they had done was when the guns from Beggar's Bush Barracks were transferred from the lorries into the courts. Since then they had been sitting around waiting for things to come to a head. They wouldn't have to wait much longer.

At around ten o'clock Dr. Jim Ryan arrived with a group of Cumann na mBan nurses. Jack strained his eyes in the failing light in an effort to see if Kathy or Helen was amongst their number, but he couldn't tell. He would have to wait until later in the evening when he re-entered the court buildings, having finished digging.

Inside, the men were preparing and cleaning rifles and machine guns, laying out spare parts for them and increasing the barricades at the windows. The nurses turned several rooms into a field hospital where an assortment of bandages, iodine, gauze and lint was arranged on several desks that were to be used as operating tables.

As soon as Free State troops had disarmed all the mines that the courts garrison had placed they drove several large Lancia trucks up to the main gates of the courts complex and parked them outside, effectively blocking the many entrances. The men began to ask for permission to fire on the soldiers who were driving the trucks, as they believed that they might contain explosives set to blow open the gates when the time was right. The officers, however, urged restraint and the trucks were put in place and the engines put out of action, so they couldn't be moved.

'They're blocking us in,' Jimmy said.

'They're planning a bloodbath, I think. It looks like they don't want to leave any escape route open to us, if we have to make a run for it,' Jack replied.

'I hear that we've sent word to Oscar Traynor and the rest of the Dublin Brigade to set up a field of snipers on the approaches to the courts to stop the Staters from advancing,' Jimmy said.

'And they've taken over some more buildings on O'Connell Street. I heard Mellows saying that they'll fight their way through to us if we need help,' Jack said, throwing a shovel-full of earth over his shoulder. As he did so he became aware of the trucks which were moving into position to the rear of the courts, bringing supplies and troops to the Bridewell, which faced the Headquarters building. Staters scurried in and out of the buildings. Lights in the upper windows revealed that sniper and machine gun positions were being taken up that would cover most of the open spaces of the court buildings, making communication between the blocks extremely difficult and dangerous. Free State troops were also taking up positions across the river, where sandbag emplacements were springing up at windows, leaving loop holes for sniper rifles and machine guns.

'I know the fight hasn't even begun, Jimmy, but I've got a bad feeling about this. We've been here over a month and their positions are already better than ours are. They've got us surrounded,' Jack said.

Once the trenches had been finished and the loose earth used to fill up sandbags, Jack and Jimmy, along with the rest of the units who were on the detail cleaned up a little and re-entered the main building for further orders. They met Barry inside.

'I've been looking for you two. I'm being sent over to O'Connell Street to deliver a message to Brugha and Traynor. Do you fancy coming with me? O'Connor told me to take two lads with me. I'll find someone else if you don't want to go,' Barry said.

'I'll go,' Jack said. 'It'll do me good to get out of this bloody place for a while.'

'And you?' Barry asked, looking at Jimmy.

'I'll come too,' Jimmy replied. If he were going to risk the streets he would be doing it in the best company he knew.

Making their way through the Four Courts the three men headed out a back entrance on to Chancery Street, passing several Free State troops who were unloading arms and equipment for use in the Bridewell. They bore the brunt of a barrage of insults that the soldiers shouted.

'Irregulars! Traitors!' one Stater shouted as he unloaded a box of ammunition from the back of a Ford truck.

'Ignore them,' Jack said in a whisper as they walked quickly away.

It was hard to keep quiet in the face of such insults, but they had been told to avoid confrontation with Free State troops by their commanding officers.

'If there's going to be trouble, it's the Staters who will have to start it,' Seán had said, aware how quickly public opinion could turn against them if they were seen to be spoiling for a fight.

They moved swiftly across the road into Greek Street, revolvers hidden under their jackets.

The Free State cordon was getting tighter as Collins' men stepped up security and mounted roadblocks across the city. Groupings of five and six soldiers stood at the bigger intersections, stopping traffic and searching vehicles. It was a trick picked up from the British Army that they were now using quite effectively against their old comrades, as they tried to gain full control of the city centre. Roaming units of the Free State Army were also stopping civilians and searching them, looking for identification and asking where they were heading.

Once the three volunteers had made their way onto Mary's Lane they headed through Smithfield Market. The bells of St. Michan's pealed almost reassuringly as the men made their way up through the market towards Green Street, from where they headed northwards to avoid a road block, until finding their way onto Parnell Street. From there it was a straight run to the Hammam Hotel on O'Connell Street and Cathal Brugha, to whom they were to deliver a message from Rory O'Connor. Barry, knowing how dangerous it was becoming on the streets, had told Jack and Jimmy the details of the message in the hope that it might still get through if he was caught. He had no reason to worry. It took them half an hour to get to the Hammam Hotel, but get there they did, and in one piece.

Republican forces had captured and held a large portion of O'Connell Street in recent days, fortifying it from above the Gresham Hotel at the most northerly point down to Cathedral Street in the south. This area quickly became known amongst the men as 'the block'.

Entering 'the block' was tricky. The younger volunteers were itching to fire their new rifles and anyone who was crazy enough to cross O'Connell Street with a gun in their hand was considered fair game. Only a warning shout to let the guards on duty know who you were could ensure the safety of those looking to enter the buildings. Jack could see the muzzles of at least fifty rifles poking through the windows of the buildings in the row. It was something of a fortress.

'Jaysus, it's here we should be, not away over in the courts,' Jack said to Barry, whilst waving to a volunteer who shouted his name from a window on the second floor of the hotel.

'Who's that?' Jimmy asked.

'I've no idea,' Jack said. 'But he seems to know me.'

The three volunteers entered the hotel foyer where they were given the once-over by the guards on duty as they asked for Brugha. Jack had never seen half of the men who were controlling 'the block', as many had come from the south side of the city and surrounding areas. Brugha turned up shortly after they arrived and nodded at Jack.

'We meet again!' Brugha said, remembering Jack from their brief chat in Mulligan's before the first convention.

'Yes sir,' Jack replied.

'Well, what is it?'

'A message from Rory O'Connor, sir,' Barry said.

'Yes?'

'He asked in the event of the courts coming under sustained attack, would it be possible to have a passage ready that we could use for escape.'

'Tell him that we've got men taking over sniping positions along the route and that it should allow for a retreat, should that become necessary. Tell him we've taken in around twenty new recruits today and we're training them. Five of them were Free State Army and have come back to us. They say there are more men thinking about doing the same. The Free Staters are taking on ex-British servicemen as officers and the Staters are being trained by Black and Tans. They don't like it one little bit, and I can't blame them,' Brugha said, turning and walking away.

The three men were preparing to leave as a familiar voice called out Jack's name. It was his cousin Terry. He too was delivering a message to the Quartermaster.

'Jaysus, Terry, you keep springing up in the most unusual places!' Jack said, happy to see his cousin.

'How's life in the GHQ?' Terry asked.

'It doesn't look too good. The rumour is that the Staters will attack later tonight,' Jack replied.

'Jaysus, that doesn't sound good. How do you think it'll go?'

'We don't know—they've built up their positions in no time at all, and we're barely able to defend ourselves after four weeks. I've got a bad feeling about it,' Jack admitted.

'I'm over in the Post Office on Marlborough Street now—it's funny—we raided it only a few weeks ago. I never thought I'd see the place again.'

'Well, at least you've got 'the block' on your back door,' Jack said. 'It's getting harder and harder to get in and out of the courts. They're putting up road blocks all over the place and slowly surrounding us.'

'We'll do all right, Jack. Keep the faith. Speaking of which—have you heard that we've all been excommunicated from the church?' Terry asked.

'We haven't!' Barry exclaimed. 'Are you sure?'

'Sure as I'll ever be,' Terry smiled.

'Those bastards are trying to break us now by using God. The Brits failed, Collins' men have failed and now this— jaysus will they not stop?' Jack wondered, seeing the worried look on Barry's face.

'Ah well, no more confession,' Jimmy said, sounding almost relieved.

'Don't worry about it, Barry,' Jack said, 'it's just another tactic—God doesn't support the British or the Free Staters any more than we do—it's a political thing and the Bishops are wrong to do this. Sure, didn't the hierarchy do the same to the Fenians, turning their backs on them when they needed them most? They'll change their tune in time, wait and see,' Jack said, hoping to ease Barry's conscience. Barry had been religious all of his life, in stark contrast to his brother Thomas, who hated all things religious. It was the one bone of contention between the two otherwise inseparable brothers.

'They're hoping to cause division in the ranks,' Terry agreed. 'It's the only reason they've done it.'

'Sure, as long as we still have people like Father Dominic and Father Albert we'll be fine, I suppose,' Barry said, referring to the two Franciscan friars who were administering the Sacraments to the Four Courts garrison.

'I'm happier without the church interfering,' Terry said, echoing the thoughts of Jack and Jimmy.

'We'd best be getting back,' Barry said, wanting to change the conversation.

'Aye, we had,' Jack agreed.

The three volunteers made their way out onto a side street and made their way back to the courts, avoiding any contact with Free State troops and checkpoints.

The cry of seagulls swooping over Smithfield Market rose as the men approached from the north. The evening light was beginning to fail as a cool wind whipped through the air. It was to be a testing time for everyone.

Chapter Eight

At around two in the morning Oscar Traynor, Commander of the Dublin Brigade arrived and held a meeting with the staff officers in the round room. Despite requests by some officers that the Executive men leave before the shooting began, they were going to stay and fight it out—whatever the outcome. Most wanted the Executive men to leave the courts to the garrison and go to the country where they could organise a general attack on Dublin. Traynor, despite agreeing with the majority, decided to back O'Connor and Mellows' position, took possession of a proclamation that O'Connor had written, and left for O'Connell Street and 'the block'. At three-forty that morning a Stater came to the main gates and handed in a letter for O'Connor. This is what it contained:

The officer in charge,

Four Courts.

I, acting under the order of the Government, hereby order you to evacuate the buildings of the Four Courts and to parade your men under arrest, without arms, on that portion of the Quays immediately in front of the Four Courts by four a.m.

Failing compliance with this order, the building will be taken by me by force, and you and all concerned with you will be held responsible for any life lost or any damage done.

By order

Thomas Ennis

O/C 2nd Eastern Division

It was finally starting.

O'Connor called the garrison to the round room under candlelight, the electricity having been cut-off an hour or two earlier. There, Father Albert gave the garrison general absolution and the men said an act of contrition, their weapons ready in their hands.

Jack saw Barry in the flicker of candlelight. He looked happy now that he had been given absolution. He could see Barry's eyes shining with a certainty he had never before seen in his comrade and it made him feel stronger inside. The whole garrison came together in that soldierly bond that happens before battle—a consolidation of emotion and purpose that is almost unstoppable.

Once the priest had finished giving absolution the men were sent back to their posts and told to wait until the Staters made the first move. The seconds passed slowly as four o'clock approached.

Jack stood at his post looking through the loopholes created for the muzzle of his rifle between the sandbags he had placed on top of a heavy oaken desk. Across the river on Winetavern Street, near the Brazen Head, he could see men moving into position with armoured cars and one or two field pieces. Jack immediately left his post and reported to Mellows who was downstairs organising the Executive men, under Ernie O'Malley's command.

'Liam, they're bringing the big guns out across the river,' Jack said.

'Artillery?' Mellows asked.

'Yes sir, eighteen-pounders I think,' Jack replied. He could see the look of shock on the faces of the Executive men and officers. Some had been in the GPO in 1916 when the British used field pieces to bombard the position. They knew what it was like to fight under sustained artillery fire. It shook the nerves each time the guns were fired, leaving some men nervous wrecks. It was the uncertainty which made the most impact on the men, one of the Executive staff officers had said—not knowing whether you would be in the wrong place at the wrong time, whether the next hit would be for you.

'Go back to your position, Jack, but keep me posted on anything else you see.' Mellows said, fixing a sling to his rifle and placing it over his shoulder.

Jack returned to his spot by the window, Jimmy standing close by, as Free State troops continued to move in with shells and gun emplacements. By now there were two heavy gun positions facing the courts—one on Winetavern Street and another on Bridgefoot Street up the quays, ensuring that there was no possibility of escape along the riverfront. Apart from the big field pieces that the Staters had no doubt borrowed from the British Army, Stokes guns were brought into place.

A Stokes gun could unleash a hail of fire unlike any other machine gun. The incessant noise of rounds hitting the walls would be enough to drive a man insane, Tom Wall told Jack, having heard stories about them from an ex-British soldier who was now in the Dublin Brigade. The only thing to do when they fire in your direction, Wall said, is to keep your head down until it stops.

'Jaysus, we're fucked,' Jimmy said. 'They've got us on all sides. It doesn't matter how many fucking trenches we dig or how much barbed wire we string up they've got us outnumbered and outgunned. I think you might have been right when you said we were going to be sacrificial lambs.'

'You never know, Jimmy. Traynor and his men are only a few streets away. If the firing gets too heavy they may be able to break through and help to get us out. Besides, it hasn't started yet, so we don't know what it's going to be like. We might scare them off,' Jack said, hopefully.

'We scared the Black and Tans off, didn't we, Jack?'
Jimmy said with a nervous smile.

Cusack turned to Jack and Jimmy, a wild look in his eyes,
and began to sing:

'Ah, come out ye Black and Tans,
Come out and fight me like a man,
Show your wife how you won medals out in Flanders;
Tell her how the IRA made you run like hell away,
From the green and lovely hills of Killeshandra...'

The atmosphere was lightened temporarily as the rest of
the men in the east wing began to sing along until a rous-
ing chorus filled the courts, defiant to the last man.

'No surrender!' a volunteer shouted, to the cheers of his
comrades.

'Up the Republic!' cried one of the officers as the bullets
began to fly. Everyone ducked in an effort to avoid the flying glass as the windows shattered. Once the firing began
in earnest the volunteers smashed out the rest of the glass
and began to return fire, seeing their bullets hit the
armour plating of the field pieces and armoured cars on
the southern bank of the Liffey. The sparks lit up the darkness.

'Aim low,' an older volunteer shouted, 'and get them in
the legs with the ricochets.'

'Mark your targets,' Seán Fitzpatrick cried as he kept an
eye on his men. 'Don't waste your ammunition. Pick a target and stay with it until you get it. I don't want three or
four of you going for the same target. There's plenty out
there for everybody,' he said with a nervous laugh. 'Jack,
Jimmy, try to keep the Stokes Gun covered—if we keep
firing at him he won't dare to raise his head and take
aim—he's got no cover. Cusack, Wall, keep your fire on

the buildings across the way. If you see the flash of a rifle, shoot at it—there's a head behind every flash. Come on lads, liven up, it's only just beginning! This is what you joined up for, now let's get the job done!' Seán cried as he marched back and forth, checking volunteers who had stopped firing or who were having problems with their rifles.

Just then the first artillery shell came whistling through the air, pounding the east wing and shaking the whole building. Plaster cracked and fell from the walls, light fittings fell from the ceiling and a huge crack appeared in the gable end wall.

'Jesus, did you feel that!' Jimmy said, filling the magazine of his Mauser rifle and returning fire, the rifle shaking in his hands.

'I hope they can't aim straight,' Jack replied, wondering what would happen if they managed to get a shell in through one of the windows.

'They'll have some British Army men over there giving them advice,' Wall said, as the Stokes gun spat out a few hundred rounds, covering the back wall of their position with fist-sized holes that raised clouds of dust. The men ducked for cover until the firing subsided and then returned fire, aiming low, as they had been told.

'I've got one!' Jimmy shouted, seeing a soldier fall to the ground clutching his knee before being dragged back behind the gun emplacements. 'That'll quieten them down a bit,' he said. Instead, it led to a barrage of fire that lasted over ten minutes, during which time the volunteers positioned at the front of the courts could do nothing but wait for it to come to an end.

'I wonder why our south side units aren't attacking the guns from the rear?' Jack said aloud.

'They're probably being kept back by more troops at

Christ Church,' Tom Wall said, switching rifles, so that the one he had been using for the last twenty minutes could cool down a little.

Jack could see the sun beginning to rise in the east over the city skyline with its greyish blues and streaks of red giving way to yellow and orange, lighting up the sky as the thud of eighteen pound shells continued to shake the east wing.

'They've knocked in the west wing's top floor already,' Con Sullivan said, delivering a box of ammo.

'Has anyone been killed?' Jack asked, hearing the dull thump of a bullet hit the sandbags in front of him.

'Not that I know of, but we've had a few wounded—one man was shot in the ankle coming back from the HQ block by snipers in St. Michan's bell tower,' Con replied. 'I'd best be getting on, I've got to do the rounds with the ammo,' he added, turning to leave, as a fresh hail of machine gun fire hit the wing, sending Con to the floor in search of cover.

'Keep that red head of yours down, Sullivan, you're making a target for those bastards across the river!' Jimmy said.

Con stood up, dusted himself off, smiled nervously and left the room, a box of ammo under his arm.

'It's beginning to get a bit hairy in here,' Jack said, taking aim at the Stokes gunner's cap, which was just visible above the armoured box he was sitting in. Jack squeezed the trigger of his rifle slowly to avoid losing his mark. His rifle recoiled. The Stokes gunner stood up briefly, held his hands to his head, and then fell from sight.

'Jesus, I think I got the gunner,' Jack said, almost shocked that he had pulled the trigger on a former comrade.

'He'd have riddled you the first chance he got,' Cusack said. 'Good shooting.'

The consequences of his actions were slowly making themselves known to Jack as he reloaded, adjusted his sights, dried the sweat from his palms and pushed the muzzle of his rifle back out through the loop in the sandbags towards a fresh target.

'Mother of God, forgive me,' he whispered, taking aim at the feet of men standing behind an armoured car, as the shells continued to wreck the solid walls of the Four Courts. The hours passed slowly.

Seán Fitzpatrick returned to the room and began barking out orders. No one had ever seen Seán this worked up and they were quick to follow his every word.

'Cusack, Wall, I want you to relieve the west wing units. They've been under heavy fire for the last few hours and need some breathing space. Jack, Jimmy, you stay where you are. Con and Barry will be up to fill the gaps. Thomas is working on a tunnel to the munitions block. Do you need anything?' Seán inquired.

'The Stokes gunners are being replaced every time we knock one out or wound them—is there any chance of getting 'The Mutineer' around to scare them back a bit?' Jimmy asked, referring to the armoured car the garrison had 'liberated' in Kildare town. It was now patrolling the open yard spaces to the rear of the main building, returning fire on Free State positions in the Bridewell and other sniper posts.

'I think the car's busy enough as it is, Jimmy. Just keep up a steady stream of fire, maybe use a rifle grenade or two—but don't go overboard, we don't have that many,' Seán replied, following Wall and Cusack from the room.

'I was going to ask him how the tunnel to the munitions dump is getting along—they put a load of inexperienced young lads over there—I'm surprised they've lasted this long,' Jack said, seeing more troops marching down Winetavern Street toward the gun emplacements. 'Quick—there's more men coming down towards the bridge,' Jack said, hoping that they might 'drop' a few more uniforms before they reached good cover.

Jimmy pushed home a fresh magazine clip and set his sights over the heads of the troops, knowing that the bullet would lose velocity and begin to fall after a few hundred feet. He had become so used to firing slightly over his target by now that he did it almost without thinking. Six shots in succession and the barrel of his Mauser rifle had begun to glow with the heat of the shots. He had been using it now for over five hours, firing at intervals, but occasionally firing round after round. The barrel was so hot that it would burn the skin if it came into contact with it, so he had learned to simply rest the barrel on the sandbags and take aim with his hands on the stock. But the heat of the barrel was now taking its toll on the weapon. Its sights were beginning to melt, rendering the gun almost useless.

Con Sullivan and Barry Murphy arrived carrying their weapons, their pockets full of ammunition.

'How is it going upstairs?' Jack asked.

'The top floor is caving in, the outside walls are shot to pieces—there's no way we could stay up there any longer,' Con said.

He was covered in a thick layer of dust, with bloody scratches making their red presence known through the ghostly mask of grey.

'The west wing is almost completely blown out of it,' Barry said. 'They're withdrawing some of the troops to the round room and sending others out to cover for them.'

'Any news on the O'Connell Street men? Are they fighting their way towards us?' Jimmy asked.

'I heard Mellows talking to O'Malley—apparently they've got as far as Capel Street, where they are holding a couple of buildings—they may yet break through—but it could take a long time,' Con said.

'How long do you think we can hold the place?' Jack asked, knowing that Con and Barry had been working in the munitions dump a few days earlier.

'Well, I'd say we have a day's ammo left, no more, if we keep firing at the rate we are. As regards food, well we thought we had enough, but that's nearly all gone too—all we have left is tea and biscuits,' Barry said.

'Well, there's always the sewers, I suppose,' Jack said. The three men looked at him confused.

'What are you talking about?' Con asked.

'O'Connor has planned an escape route that we can use if it comes down to it. The sewer runs from the building across a couple of streets where we can get out and make a run for it when the time comes,' Jack said, knowing that this would cheer the men up a little.

'It's nice to know they've got something planned for us,' Jimmy remarked. 'I was beginning to feel a little nervous.'

'Me too,' Con said. 'What we are doing now goes against everything that we've ever been taught. I don't understand it.'

'You're not alone,' Jack replied. 'I've been picking Liam's brain on this for the past few days—he says that it's more of a stand than a fight, but I think he's changing his mind—he's hoping for support to arrive from the country.'

'That sounds familiar,' Barry said. 'The countrymen always turn up, but they usually arrive too bloody late. If we don't get some relief soon then I reckon the place is going to fall.'

A burst of Stokes fire hit the front walls and masonry began to fly, sending chips of stone through the air. Everyone in the room ducked as the bullets entered the window and slammed into the rear walls, removing what little plaster was now left, and raising a choking cloud of dust that invaded the eyes, nose and throat.

'Jaysus, how many men do they have for that fucking Stokes gun?' Jimmy asked.

'They have a damned sight more men than we do, that's for sure,' Con replied, taking aim and firing at a position in a building across the river.

Evening was approaching fast and so far none of the garrison had been killed. There had been five or six wounded and dozens of close calls, but loss of life had thus far been avoided.

Seán Fitzpatrick arrived looking gaunt and withdrawn. The fight was beginning to take its toll on everyone. Most hadn't slept for over twenty-four hours and there were not enough men to allow proper relief, so the prospect of getting any sleep was quite remote. One or two men had fallen asleep at their posts from sheer exhaustion, only to be woken by their officers and sent to another post.

'The west wing has nearly fallen. We've been laying mines in the passages and putting down bobbins of barbed wire and barricades but the Staters are making headway. Most of the west wing has been blown to bits,' Seán said, the power gone from his voice.

'Well, they haven't got the east wing yet, sir,' Jack said, hoping to lift Seán's spirits somewhat.

'You're a good man,' Seán said, putting his hand on Jack's shoulder.

'What have you heard about the munitions block?' Barry asked. 'Have they relieved those young lads who were holding it?'

'I think they sent some men across to help them out, but they're getting it from all sides now, what with the Bridewell and the sniper positions around the place,' Seán said. 'The tunnel still isn't finished.'

'Any news on Traynor's men coming from O'Connell

Street?' Con asked.

'The last I heard they were pinned down on Capel Street—I don't think they're going to get through.'

'Are there any plans for a retreat?' Jimmy asked.

'Not yet, Jimmy. It's too early for that.'

'How much longer do you think we can hold out?' Jack asked, wondering if Barry's assessment had been right.

'I don't know, Jack. I don't know,' Seán said, walking away.

Jack had never seen Seán like that. He was always so full of life, so full of hope, always offering leadership when it was required. He knew now that the whole episode was doomed to failure. It didn't inspire confidence.

The heavy guns started to pound the east wing once again, rocking the entire building each time a round slammed home, creating craters in the outside wall and in some places punching holes right through. The ceiling was beginning to give way and large blocks of masonry were falling on the men, who were doing their best to return fire in an effort to stop the incessant pounding. Jimmy threw his rifle to one side, the sights now completely useless, and picked up a Lee Enfield Speed which Con had offered him. As he was loading the rifle, a shell hit the window and threw him across the room and against the wall. The other three volunteers were also hit, but not badly. Con had some shrapnel in his arm, Barry had been hit on the head by a chunk of stone and Jack had been thrown back by the force of the blast, but wasn't injured. When the dust began to settle, the volunteers made their way over to Jimmy, who was slumped against the wall.

'Jimmy! Jimmy, are you all right?' Jack asked, cradling his friend's head on his lap. 'Are you all right?'

Jimmy was bleeding heavily on the right side of his face and blood was trickling from his ear. He couldn't hear a thing. Jack opened his trench coat and searched his body for puncture wounds. There were none. It appeared that he had just been hit in the head.

'Con, go and get a nurse, will you?' Jack asked.

Con ran from the room and returned a minute later with a young Cumann na mBan woman armed with a bundle of bandages and a bottle of iodine. She quickly went to work on Jimmy's bleeding head-wound in an effort to stem the flow of blood. When she had finished dressing the wound she asked Jack and Barry to carry Jimmy downstairs to the makeshift field hospital where Dr. Ryan was treating casualties.

Jimmy seemed to be drifting in and out of consciousness as they carried him down the stairs towards the infirmary. On arrival, another nurse told them to place Jimmy on a desk and leave the rest to them.

'Jimmy, you'll be all right now,' Jack said. 'Don't worry about a thing, do you hear?' Jimmy's eyes flickered as he regained consciousness briefly. A painful smile glanced across his face as he saw his old friend Jack looking down at him. Jack could feel the tears welling in his eyes as he turned to leave his old friend.

'Come on, there's nothing more we can do. They'll take good care of him,' Barry said in an effort to reassure Jack. He knew they had been best friends for over ten years and he could see the tears welling in Jack's eyes. 'He'll be fine, Jack. Sure that bastard has a hard enough head on him—I know, I've punched it often enough!' Barry said with a smile.

Jack smiled too. 'The war is over for Jimmy,' he said, thinking of the first time they had met. It was at a Fianna na hÉireann recruitment day and the two had become friends immediately. They had been almost inseparable since then.

'Aye, and it'll be over for us too if we don't try to find some way out of this place,' Barry said, seeing the Executive men holding a meeting in the round room as they headed back to their posts.

'What do you think they're planning?' Jack asked as they climbed the stairs.

'God only knows. I'm beginning to lose faith in them, to tell you the truth. The only decent brains amongst them are Mellows and O'Malley but they can't make all the decisions on their own, they have to toe the line like everyone else,' Barry said.

'They're all good men, Barry,' Jack said. 'They're doing their best, but they're just not used to fighting this way, that's all. We're a guerrilla army, not a regular army. That's where the battle lines should have been drawn. We've bitten off more than we can chew and now we're going to pay for it with our lives.'

'Do you think they'll fight on to the end?' Barry asked.

'I don't know. Some of the lads are already wondering when we'll surrender—they say it's just a matter of time, that there's no way we can hold out. I'm beginning to wonder myself,' Jack said, seeing men take refuge in the hallways as the outside walls gave way and exposed the rooms to continuous fire from across the river.

When the two volunteers got to the first floor they found Con in the hallway.

'Are you alright, Con?' Jack asked.

'We got another direct hit just after you left—the outside walls have given way and there's no cover in there anymore. We'll have to go down to the ground floor,' Con replied, clutching his arm in obvious pain. There was a dark stain of blood on his shirt and drops were running down to his left hand in which he clasped his Webley revolver.

'You should go and get a proper dressing on that wound, Con,' Barry said

'I'm fine, boy, I'm fine,' Con replied. 'Now, let's get down those stairs before this bloody hallway gets a hit.'

The three men headed down to the round room where they saw the commander of the munitions block and his men enter the main building. One or two were badly wounded from having to cross the yards under sniper fire.

'Looks like the munitions block has fallen,' Jack observed.

'It's on fire,' one of the volunteers said. 'It could blow at any minute. We tried to keep the explosives away from the flames but they just kept spreading. I'd keep as far away from the munitions block as I could if I were you.'

The young men from the munitions block looked shattered. Almost two days without food or sleep under constant fire had taken its toll. Most of the men were now in a numbed state, not even flinching when stray bullets ricocheted around them.

Plans were being made at the behest of the garrison doctor, according to Seán Fitzpatrick, to have the wounded removed. This, Seán told Jack and Barry, would mean a slight lull in the shooting to allow for their removal.

'I want you two to keep the hallways into the west wing covered, there are Staters in there already and they're trying to move in on our position,' Seán instructed Jack and Barry.

'Is there any sign of Thomas?' Barry asked. He hadn't seen his brother for over twenty-four hours.

'He was in the digging party constructing the tunnel to the munitions block, but I presume they've been called back now that the block has been evacuated,' Seán said.

'But I haven't seen him, sir. Can I check that he got back?' Barry asked.

'Of course, just hurry it up—we don't want to lose all of the west wing.'

'Thanks,' Barry said gratefully before heading downstairs to the cellars towards the tunnel mouth, Jack at his side.

In the cellars they came across eight volunteers covered in mud and smelling to high heaven. One of the eight stepped forward and spoke.

'Ah, lads, can you smell the clean fresh country air.' It was Thomas, attempting to wipe the mud from his face.

'That's shite,' Jack replied, seeing Barry's relief on meeting his brother.

'True enough, we punctured a sewage pipe in the digging,' Thomas replied

'Well, you lads should get as far from that blasted tunnel as you can, the munitions block is on fire and they expect it to blow any minute,' Barry said, hoping the men would heed his warning.

'But there's still four men in there digging,' Thomas said, looking into the mouth of the tunnel. 'I'm going in after them—the rest of you go on out of it, we'll be up in a minute.'

Barry grabbed Thomas' arm tightly and looked him in the eye. 'Don't go playing the hero,' he said.

'Don't worry. I'll be back in a minute,' Thomas replied with a smile. It made him feel good knowing that his older brother was looking out for him.

The remaining men stood fast while Thomas entered the tunnel on his hands and knees in search of his comrades, whose oil lamps could be seen flickering in the distance. All of a sudden a rumbling sound filled the air and a thick cloud of dust emerged from the tunnel.

'The tunnel's collapsing,' Barry said, moving quickly toward its entrance. Jack and another volunteer held him back.

'There's no use going in just yet. Wait until we hear from Thomas,' Jack said, in an effort to calm him down.

Barry struggled free and entered the tunnel, disappearing into the dust. Time stood still.

A muffled blast could be heard and another cloud of dust emerged from the tunnel mouth.

Jack moved forward and called out.

'Barry? Thomas? Can you hear me?' There was no reply.

'Should we go in after them?' Con wondered aloud.

'Give them another minute,' Jack replied, his eyes fixed on the mouth of the tunnel.

The sound of shouting and frantic digging came from the tunnel. Jack got down on his hands and knees and crawled in. The air was filled with a suffocating dust, while the floor of the tunnel was wet with mud. He couldn't see a thing. The sound of rocks being moved came from up ahead, as parts of the tunnel wall fell in on top of him. He could hear Con calling his name from behind, asking him to get out.

'Barry? Thomas? Can you hear me?' Jack shouted again. This time he heard a faint voice coming from up ahead.

'It's all right. One of the lads got stuck. We're coming out.'

Jack turned and crawled back out into the basement where Con stood waiting with the rest of the digging party.

Two minutes later Barry, Thomas and the four-man digging party emerged from the tunnel looking relieved. Jack felt like he had aged ten years in those few minutes. The men made their way back up to ground level, getting as far from the munitions block as was possible.

Barry, Thomas and Jack headed over to the corridors connecting the west wing and built several barricades laced with bobbins of barbed wire, while Wall and

Cusack, who had been there for some time, checked the rooms ahead with the Thompson sub-machine guns they had been given by an officer. As each room was declared clear, the men moved forward. As they reached the last safe spot on the corridor a large blast shook the entire building and the sky, which could be seen through holes in the roof, was filled with smoke and burning papers that caught the wind and twirled haphazardly in the air.

'That was the munitions block,' Jack explained to Wall and Cusack, who didn't know that it was on fire.

'So that's the end of the ammo?' Cusack asked.

'All we have left is what each man has on him and maybe another box or two with the officers in the round room,' Barry replied.

As he did so a rifle grenade burst in one of the rooms behind them sending shrapnel through the closed door and into the hall, embedding itself in the wall.

'Come on, let's start making our way back. It looks like we've got company,' Jack said, as a burst of machine gun fire tore plaster off the walls of the corridor up ahead.

The men crouched low and moved back the way they had come, creating as many obstacles along the path as they could in the hope of slowing the advance of the Staters. Wall and Cusack stopped momentarily to return fire with their Thompson guns. As they reached a connecting corridor and made their way across an open space the sound of shouting could be heard.

'Hold it right there boys, you're prisoners,' came the voice.

Jack turned around briefly as they began to run for cover, seeing four men in Free State uniforms standing on the balcony above, guns at the ready.

'Run for it,' Jack screamed to Wall and Cusack, who were behind them.

As the two men ran across the open space they were shot dead by Staters who opened fire with a machine gun. Jack, now under cover, swore loudly, withdrew his Browning LE automatic, stepped into the open and emptied his magazine at the soldiers, hitting one in the chest and clipping another, before Barry pulled him back under cover.

'Jaysus, Jack, will you be careful, it's bad enough that they got Wall and Cusack without putting yourself on the block too,' Barry said, clearly shaken by what he had just witnessed.

'We'd best get back to the round room,' Thomas said, hearing footsteps on the stairs ahead of them.

The three volunteers moved swiftly down the corridor towards the centre of the main building. There under, what was left of the huge dome of the rotunda, the entire garrison was assembled, waiting for further instructions as the wounded were being carried out to waiting ambulances.

Mellows and O'Connor were busy talking. Jack could see that Mellows was not happy with what O'Connor was suggesting.

'I wonder what's going to happen now?' Thomas asked.

'God only knows,' Barry replied.

O'Connor got up, stood on a bench, called for silence and began to speak.

'We have been asked to surrender by the Dublin Brigadier, Oscar Traynor, as he has been unable to break through to us. He believes that our posts in O'Connell Street and around the city will be in a better position if we surrender, allowing them to fight on and not be distracted by what is happening here. I know some of you want to surrender too,' O'Connor said sternly.

As he did so a cry of 'No surrender!' came up from the floor followed by the stamping of boots.

'We are not in a position to continue the fight. We have no food and very little ammunition. I know some of you would like to fight to the end, but I think the sensible thing to do right now is to surrender. Standby for further orders,' O'Connor finished, getting down from the bench. He headed over to Ernie O'Malley and Liam Mellows.

'Well, that's it,' Jack said. 'Another one lost.'

'It's not over yet,' Barry said. 'What about those sewers?'

'They're flooded by the Liffey tide,' a volunteer close by said. 'There's no way out, we've been completely surrounded.'

'Well, we didn't do too badly,' Thomas said. 'How many casualties?'

'I don't know,' Jack said.

An hour passed by. Passages to the round room were held firm by the remaining volunteers until O'Connor issued orders to strip and destroy weapons and to assemble in units.

Jack stood waiting for further orders, his heart sinking with every breath. A quiet gloom descended on the men. One or two volunteers wept openly as they destroyed their new weapons. The fight was over.

Chapter Nine

O'Malley handled the surrender. He called the men to attention before giving the order to march out onto the banks of the Liffey. Outside, Free State troops and officers waited for them.

Jack, Con, Barry and Thomas lined up along Inns Quay with their comrades, a feeling of defeat in their hearts. A Free State officer called the men to attention. The response was a wave of insults and jeering. In an effort to show the men's discipline in defeat, Ernie O'Malley called the men to attention. They immediately fell into line and awaited further orders.

As a newspaper photographer appeared from beyond Whitworth Bridge and began to set up his tripod opposite the lines of men, O'Malley marched up to him and told him in no uncertain terms what he would do if the man attempted to take a photo. The man backed off, his tripod under his arm.

Under instruction of the Free State officer in charge of the surrender, O'Malley ordered the men into groups of four and sent them marching along the quay, up Church Street and into Jameson's Distillery. Mellows and O'Connor led the men into the open, high-walled yard.

'Well, that's that,' Barry said, seeing the high walls. 'There's no way in hell we could get out of here.'

'Where there's a will there's a way,' Con said, keeping his eyes peeled.

The sound of a gathering crowd filled the air. Shouts of support came over the walls. In response, some of the men passed their holsters out through the barred windows to people they knew for safekeeping.

'It's a shame they haven't laid on a little whiskey for us,' Thomas said, the smell of sewage still clinging to his clothes.

'It's more than whiskey I need right now,' Jack replied, checking under his trench coat for the Browning automatic he had hidden.

The men had not been searched. Although they had been given general orders to destroy their guns, a few volunteers were still carrying in the hope that it gave them the possibility of escape.

'I wonder how long they're going to hold us here?' Barry asked, distractedly.

'I'd say they'll move us up the road to Mountjoy soon— this can't be anything more than a temporary holding spot,' Con said, trying to work out an escape route.

Word quickly filtered through that O'Malley had escaped with another few men by walking past some guards and entering an office that had a connecting door to the street outside. Bursts of gunfire could be heard in the distance, and Jack imagined the Staters trying to catch up with the escapees. They would have a hard time, he thought, having heard tales of O'Malley's sharp mind and exploits during the Tan War. He was sure to make good his escape.

Jack sat down on an overturned whiskey barrel feeling the sharp edges of the pistol pressing into his hip bone, secure in the knowledge that if any attempt was made to rush the guards, he would be ready. In the meantime though, he thought it might be a good idea to keep his head down and wait for the fuss, which O'Malley's escape had caused, to die down. Security had been increased and there was no immediate chance of escape.

'Stick together lads,' Jack said. 'If we are being moved make sure we all go together, right? I have a wee surprise for you.'

The three volunteers looked at Jack with wonder in their eyes. They could tell he had something up his sleeve, or perhaps, as they reasoned, under his coat. Con smiled.

'I wouldn't doubt ya boy!'

Jack returned the smile, gave a conspiratorial wink and looked away, lest he attract unwanted attention. The rest of the unit had destroyed their weapons as they had been ordered by staff officers. They would rather see good weapons destroyed than in the hands of the Staters. But Jack had become so attached to his Browning automatic that he didn't have the heart to dismantle and destroy it. He wondered how O'Malley could have thrown his Parabellum into the Liffey when they were on the quays. Just the feel of the gun in the waistband of his trousers lifted his spirits and gave him hope. The power, the strength, the conviction, it was all there, waiting to be put to use when the time came.

The men were put into rooms that were acting as holding cells for the night. Enjoying their first real meal in three days, the volunteers attempted to bring some life back into the proceedings and organised a sing song whilst telling stories of how many uniforms they had been able to get a shot at during the Four Courts battle. Some of the men were wondering what would happen to the Republican officers in charge. They had already been separated from the rest of the men.

As the evening light began to fade the drifting smoke and smell of burning from the Four Courts began to clear. It was soon replaced by the smells of the distillery and the

Guinness brewery up the river. The men attempted to get some sleep on the cold stone floors of the distillery.

Woken early next morning by the pealing of St. Michan's bells, Jack and the rest of the unit cleaned themselves up as best they could and waited for something to happen. It was a fine July morning and the sun was beating down hard on the flagstones that lined the yard where they were being held. Seagulls drifted carelessly on the wind, hovering, diving and climbing as the fancy took them.

The men, most beginning to accept their imprisonment, looked up at the birds longingly, wishing they could be up there with them, totally free, rising above their recent battles. It was as if the spirits of their dead comrades were hovering overhead to remind them of what they were fighting for, what they had to continue fighting for.

As ten o'clock came, Free State troops, accompanied by an officer, approached the men and told them that they were to be moved to Mountjoy Gaol. For this purpose, he said, squads of six should be formed for transport in the prison wagons. But as there were only two available, the transfer of prisoners was likely to go on all day.

'I think we should try to get in on the first few transports,' Jack said. 'That way we have some hope of escaping before anyone else tries it and ruins it for us.'

'Good thinking, Jack. I'll go and get Seán,' Barry said, walking off into the crowd.

'That makes five—we need six,' Con said, looking around for someone he knew.

'What about Frank Hourihan?' Thomas offered, seeing the man across the yard. 'He's a good man in a scrap—we fought together one time out in Lucan.'

'Any objections?' Jack asked, looking at Con, who shook his head.

Barry returned with Seán, whose interest had been sparked by what Barry had whispered to him. 'Jack has something in his trousers that he'd like you to see,' Barry had said. At first Seán thought that he was just pulling his leg, but it quickly dawned on him what Barry was trying to say in the presence of one or two other officers, with whom he didn't want to share his little bit of news.

'Well, Jack, disobeying orders again?' Seán said with a smile.

'It's such a nice piece, Seán, I couldn't destroy it,' Jack replied, unsure if he was going to be reprimanded or thanked.

'Well done, lad,' Seán said. The light of hope reappeared in his eyes. 'We may get out of this kip yet.'

'They're getting parties of six together for the prison wagons. They only have two guards in the front of each,' Jack said. 'It should be easy enough.'

'Who's coming with us?' Seán asked.

'Well, the unit comes first, Seán, that's only fair—and we thought we'd take Frank Hourihan too—he's a good man in a fight, according to Thomas,' Jack replied.

'I'd prefer it if we took an officer—the men outside need as much help as they can get,' Seán said, looking over at Hourihan, who still hadn't been told it was his lucky day. Hourihan was a stocky little man with a body as solid as the train tracks he helped to lay in his previous life.

'Who did you have in mind?' Jack asked.

'No one in particular,' Seán replied, looking around him. 'It's your call, Jack—it's your game and I'll go along with your choice,' Seán said.

'So, is everyone happy with Frank Hourihan then?' Jack asked.

A succession of nods and grunts told him that they were.

Thomas approached Hourihan and took him to one side. The lads laughed as they saw a broad smile break across his face.

'Looks like we have made somebody's day,' Con said with a grin.

'We'd best make our way up to the front of the queue,' Seán said, taking command once again. The men were glad to see Seán back to his old self and followed willingly. They would have followed him to hell and back if he had asked. To some extent they already had.

With the Free State officer somewhat anxious to get the prisoners moving, the two wagons had been drawn up close to the gates, where a heavily armed party of troops stood guard. Seán stepped forward and asked the officer in charge when the transport would begin.

'Soon,' the officer replied, without looking at him.

The minutes passed as the guards made the wagons ready for the prisoners and then prepared to open the gates, their guns trained on the lines of men.

'Right,' came the voice of the officer in charge of the transport, 'I want you to fall into groups of six.'

Seán stood forward, the five men behind him, and nodded at the officer. 'It is Mick Ryan isn't it?'

The officer took a long look at Seán's face and began to smile on recognising him. 'Jaysus, Seán, you're looking rough,' the officer replied.

'The food you're serving here isn't the best,' Seán replied, the two men laughing together.

'I haven't seen you in over a year,' the officer said.

'Well, you know, we've been somewhat busy over the last few months.'

'Are these your men?'

'Aye, they are. Could we all travel together? I don't want

them broken up,' Seán said, the officer taking a good look at each of the men standing before him.

'No problem, Seán. No hard feelings eh?'

'No, no hard feelings, Mick. Good luck,' Seán replied, leading the five volunteers into the back of the prison wagon and instructing them to sit down. The doors were closed and locked as the driver started the engine, a Stater riding shotgun beside him with a rifle on his lap.

'We should wait until we're up past Bolton Street before me make a move,' Seán whispered. 'That way we can work our way down to O'Connell Street and rejoin the Brigade.'

The men nodded in agreement as the wagon pulled away from the distillery and headed up Church Street before turning right onto North King Street.

'You lads put up a bloody good show in the Four Courts,' the Stater said, a smile on his face. 'For a while there some of the lads were going to try to join you.'

'I've heard that a lot of you lads are unhappy with who's being brought in to train you,' Seán said, taking a dig at the uniform in front.

'Aye, they've brought in ex-British Army officers and a few Black and Tans—the men don't like it one little bit. They're hard bastards,' the guard said, as the wagon bounced its way onto Bolton Street.

'But they're never as hard as us,' Jack said, removing the Browning from beneath his trench coat and flicking off the safety catch.

'That's true you know, we made the bastards run during the Tan Fight, didn't we?' the Stater said with a smile.

'You're not wrong,' Seán said, nodding at Jack, who levelled the pistol at the Stater's head. 'Now, would you kindly stop the wagon and let us out?'

'What do you think you're playing at?' the man asked on seeing the pistol pointing at his head.

'We're not playing,' Seán said. 'And my man here has a very itchy trigger finger, so you'd best stop the wagon now.'

The driver pulled the wagon over to the side of the road and got out to unlock the wagon, while Jack held the Stater at gunpoint. The six men got out and Con disarmed the guard.

'No hard feelings eh?' Con said with a laugh as the driver made a run for it across the street, quickly followed by the guard.

'Well, it looks like we've got transport if we want it,' Seán remarked.

'It'll be easier getting through the road blocks in this yoke than on foot, I suppose,' Jack replied.

'Right so, Barry, will you do the honours?' Seán asked, getting into the guard's seat while the rest of the men got into the back of the wagon and closed the door.

'Yes sir! Where would you like to go sir? Sandymount or Dollymount?' Barry replied with a laugh, referring to two popular beaches in Dublin.

'O'Connell Street, if you don't mind—but take the back streets down by North Cumberland Street and we can approach from the rear,' Seán said with a smile, cradling the rifle on his lap.

Pulling the prison wagon up on Marlborough Street, to the rear of 'the block', the six men got out, waving a near-white shirt that Barry had been wearing, in an effort to ward off the bullets that were coming from the buildings up ahead. As they approached a doorway a muffled countryman's voice could be heard from the other side.

'Who are ye? What do ye want?'

'We're members of the Dublin Brigade, we've escaped after the Four Courts battle,' Seán said. 'I'm Commandant Seán Fitzpatrick—have a word with your officers and get us in off the street, there are snipers everywhere.'

The door opened slowly and the countryman took a long look at the men assembled in front of him.

'Right, in ye come—but I'll have to take them guns off of ye,' he said, scratching his head as a second volunteer took their weapons to another room and got an officer. The officer returned with the second volunteer and introduced himself.

'I'm Paddy Slattery, Adjutant to the Commander of 'the block',' the man said.

'Commandant Seán Fitzpatrick of the Dublin Brigade. We've escaped from the Jameson Distillery and we wanted to get back into the fight,' Seán said, looking the man up and down and wondering if he had met him before.

Slattery's eyes opened a little wider as if he had only just understood who they were.

'I thought you were new recruits,' Slattery laughed. 'Sorry about this. I'll take you up to Commandant Traynor right away,' he said, looking rather sheepish.

'No problem,' Seán replied. 'But we'd like our weapons back,' he said, knowing how attached Jack had become to his Browning pistol.

Once they had their guns, Slattery took the men on a circuitous route through connecting passages and tunnels that led in a haphazard line to the Hammam Hotel on O'Connell Street. Once they had reached the second floor Slattery asked the men to wait in the hallway as he went into Traynor's room with the news. A moment later Traynor, accompanied by Cathal Brugha, stepped out into the hall and greeted Seán like a long-lost brother.

'Jesus, Seán, how did you manage to get out of the Four Courts?' Traynor asked, a smile on his face.

'They moved us over to Jameson's after the surrender and Jack here still had a gun with him, so we used it to escape while they were moving us to Mountjoy,' Seán said.

'Did anyone else escape? What about Liam and Rory and the rest of the Executive men?' Brugha asked, looking at the six men assembled in front of him.

'They're still being held. They were separated from the main bunch of volunteers just after we were brought in—but Ernie O'Malley managed to escape,' Seán said.

'I'd never doubt that he did!' Traynor replied. 'He's a good man.'

'You put up a good show in the Four Courts, lads,' Brugha said. 'They had help with the guns, you know. The British gave them to Collins when he agreed to go against us and they gave him officers to train the gunners, too.'

'Artillery is a hard thing to fight against,' Seán said, the two leaders nodding in agreement.

'So you're back in the fight then?' Brugha asked.

'Yes sir,' Seán said with a smile. It seemed as though his raison d'être had returned.

'Right, well, we need a few men over in the Gresham. I don't suppose any of you lads were chefs in your previous lives?' Traynor asked. The men shook their heads. 'That's a pity, we haven't eaten anything resembling a decent meal since we took the buildings. Your men can take part of the second floor to the front of the building on O'Connell Street. I'd like to have a chat with you first though,' Traynor said, effectively dismissing Seán's men.

'Can we get a few more guns for the lads?' Seán asked.

'I'll have someone take up a few rifles shortly,' Brugha said.

Jack, Thomas, Con, Barry and their new-found friend, Frank Hourihan, made their way through the cleared passageways that linked the buildings and soon found themselves in a rather well decorated room on the second floor of the Gresham Hotel.

'Jaysus they have it sweet over here, don't they?' Con said.

'Well, it beats the hell out of sleeping on stone floors or auld desks,' Frank Hourihan replied.

'What's happening across the street?' Jack asked, seeing Barry's cautious glances at the street below.

'They've got their armoured cars and field pieces across on the corner of Henry Street and they're pointing this way,' Barry replied.

'That's all we need—more artillery coming in the windows,' Thomas commented.

'Well, we have a good height advantage here and they can't really get troops up to our positions on foot without us taking pot-shots at them, so we're fairly safe for now,' Jack said, hearing a bullet whiz past his head. It embedded itself in the back wall of the hotel room. 'Looks like they've got snipers across the street too—we'd best keep our heads down.'

A volunteer carrying five Lee Enfield rifles arrived and gave them to the men, another delivered a box of ammunition with the message that that was all they would be getting for the foreseeable future, and not to waste it.

Con shook his head. 'Is there a shortage of ammunition?' he asked the young volunteer.

'It's being rationed. There's still a good bit left, but they're being careful with it,' the young man replied. He could be no more than sixteen, Con thought, remembering how young some of the other volunteers in the building had seemed as they made their way through to the Gresham.

'What are our chances of getting some food or drink?' Thomas asked.

'The bar was raided the day we took the buildings, but the kitchen is working and they have lots of tinned food and bread. We have one or two volunteers who used to work for a bakery—they're baking fresh bread in the ovens every day, so we're mostly eating bread and soup,' the young volunteer replied.

'So there's no drink to be had?' Thomas asked again in the hope of getting a better answer.

'You might find some in the store room below the bar, but Commandant Traynor put a guard on it to stop the men from getting drunk after the bar was raided,' he replied.

'I suppose there's no chance of room service?' Con Sullivan remarked.

'Is a nice soft bed not enough for you?' Thomas replied as a hail of bullets entered the room, sending the volunteers to the floor in search of cover.

'Right,' Jack said, 'enough messing around, let's get a barricade up against these windows and start spotting their sniping positions. Seeing as we're here we may as well get on with it.'

The men began to move the large wooden dressing table and wardrobe over to the windows and brought chairs over so they could sit at their posts and take aim in relative comfort. When the barricades were sufficiently high the men began to take shots at the buildings opposite in an effort to draw the fire of the Free State snipers. They also fired an occasional shot in the direction of the Lancia armoured cars and gun emplacement on the corner of Henry Street and O'Connell Street.

Jack's mind was all over the place. He hadn't had time to think in the past few days, what with all of the excitement and fighting that had been going on. It was if he had become a fighting machine unable to think about himself. He could only think of the task in hand and how he might best fulfil his duties. Earlier questions about what they were doing, the way they were doing it and their right to bear arms had all but disappeared in the heat of battle. His anger had grown immeasurably after British artillery had been trained on the Four Courts and Wall and Cusack were shot down in cold blood by advancing Staters. Any doubts he had had up to that point were now erased. His only desire was to fight to the best of his ability. The new surroundings, the general feeling that they could still win out, given time and reinforcements from the country, outweighed his earlier feelings of impending doom.

'It's the same gun they had over on Winetavern Street opposite our spot in the courts,' Barry said, looking out across O'Connell Street.

'Our old friend,' Thomas said sarcastically.

'They don't need it down there anymore,' Jack replied coldly.

Seán arrived an hour later, pleased to see that the men had erected barricades and were actively working on reducing the number of snipers across the road.

'Jack, I've got a little news for you and Barry,' Seán said. 'Someone must be praying for the two of you!'

'What is it?' Jack asked.

Barry turned to face Seán.

'Your girls are here working as nurses,' Seán said with a smile. 'I told them where you're positioned, so they'll probably turn up if they get a little time off.'

Jack and Barry smiled broadly on hearing the news. 'Are they all right?' Jack inquired.

'They look as fine as you've ever seen them,' Seán replied, as another hail of gunfire came through the windows. The dust of bullet-shattered bricks filled the room and the splintered window frames began to fall apart.

'So, what's our position like?' Con asked, keeping his head down. 'It looks a bit better than the Four Courts, but they're already rationing ammunition.'

'They're just being careful after what happened to us in the courts. They're learning from our mistakes. I had a good chat with Traynor and Brugha and I think we might have some support coming from the south shortly. The Tipperary lads are supposed to be here soon,' Seán replied.

'Do you think we can hold out long enough?' Jack asked.

'This place is like a rabbit warren—there are more tunnels and passages than you could ever dream of—it'll take them at least a week to make any sort of headway at all, I'd say,' Seán said, looking around the room. 'Seeing as we have a bed, we can take turns on it—but I suggest we move it away from the windows. Some of you could do with a bit of sleep—you look like ghosts,' he added, looking at Jack.

'So, what positions are we still holding around the city?' Barry asked.

'We've got snipers all over the place and they're slowing up the advance of the Staters—that's why the big guns have only just been brought in—the snipers have been keeping them away from Henry Street for the past two days. But it looks like they've finally broken through, so we can expect the real fight to begin soon. We're still holding most of Gardiner Street and Marlborough Street, which could be useful if we have to make a quick retreat,' Seán said. 'But I think the general idea is to hold out as long as possible and wait for the country boys to arrive.'

'Are there any moves being made to stop the fighting? Is Collins still set on the Treaty?' Con asked.

'Aye, it looks that way. Dev is here in 'the block'—he rejoined the Dublin Brigade as a volunteer and is supposed to be doing some work on trying to reach an agreement.

Though God only knows what he's offering them,' Seán said, thinking of de Valera's previous gestures. 'The time for politics has passed.'

The last few days had seen several attempts to bring about a cease-fire. Apart from de Valera's attempts to broker a cease-fire, the Archbishop of Dublin, Maud Gonne and leaders of the Labour Party had all been busy in an effort to stop the fighting. Unfortunately the Free State government had, on each occasion, demanded that the Republican forces surrender their arms. This was totally unacceptable to the Republican leadership.

The sound of heavy machine gun fire could be heard shattering the bricks of the outside walls as two Rolls Royce Whippet armoured cars drove up and down O'Connell Street, raking the buildings with their Vickers guns as the artillery was being set up. The larger Lancia armoured cars were being used once again to provide cover for the gun crews as they trained their weapon on 'the block'. At present there was only one eighteen-pounder and two Lancia armoured cars, but according to Seán more guns were being brought into place up by Parnell Street as the Free State forces drew their net tighter on the city centre.

'How long do you think these buildings will stand up to the artillery?' Jack asked.

'I don't know. These walls aren't as thick as those over in the courts, so I expect they'll not handle too many hits before crumbling. You'll all have to take extra care when you see the gun being trained on you—even if it means leaving your posts briefly—it's better than losing men,' Seán said.

The incessant shelling in the courts had almost driven the men insane at one point as the walls began to give way and crumble under the onslaught of firepower. The repetitive thudding of rounds as they hit the masonry, coupled with the cracking plaster and the flying shards of glass had made some men shake in fear of their lives, while others recited the rosary as they continued to return fire. Jack was expecting the coming days to be the same as those in the courts.

Later that evening Kathy and Helen arrived with some food and a couple of bottles of stout that they had managed to get from the storeroom. Jack looked relieved to see his girl and his sister in one piece.

'Oh, Jack!' Kathy said, hugging him with all her might. 'I heard about the fall of the Four Courts—I thought you'd be in Mountjoy by now. Is everyone all right?'

'We managed to get away. How have you been? Have you heard anything from home?' Jack asked, opening the bottle of stout she had given him. It tasted like nectar must taste to the bees, he thought, feeling the layers of dust in his throat slowly give way to the bubbling stout as it bit at the back of his throat.

'Ma's fine,' Helen said, as she hugged Barry.

'Everyone is fine,' Kathy said. 'They've evacuated a lot of people from the tenements, but your mother wouldn't go. My parents and the rest of street are staying put too, despite what the Parish Priest said.'

'If you see Ma before I do, tell her to take care,' Jack said to his sister, Helen.

'Has anyone been hurt?' Kathy asked again, wiping the dust from Jack's face with a damp cloth. She took a step back and looked him over, checking that he was all right, like he had said.

'Jimmy was hit hard in the head—he was taken from the courts by the ambulance—but they said he'll be fine,' Jack said, looking into Kathy's eyes. 'I love you,' he whispered into her ear. She tightened her grip around his waist.

'We can't stay for long,' Kathy said. 'We've got a lot of casualties to attend to and there aren't all that many nurses here at the moment. They're trying to get some more sent in.'

'Can you come again tomorrow?' Jack asked.

'I'll try my best,' she replied, as she and Helen prepared to leave.

Helen smiled at Jack. 'Don't go doing anything stupid now, do you hear me?'

'Look after yourself, and Kathy too,' he said. He felt strangely empty as he watched them leave, and wondered if he would ever see them again.

Jack was weary. It was now the sixth of July and he had been fighting almost non-stop since the twenty-eighth of June. In that time he had seen his best friend badly injured by a direct hit and he had also seen Wall and Cusack shot down at close range by the Staters. His mind whirred at pace as he took two hours rest, hearing the bursts of rifle and machine gun fire continue in his absence. It was as though he no longer mattered. The whole episode had begun to seem pointless. What were they trying to achieve? How were they trying to achieve it? The Republic was still in his mind, but it seemed more distant, less tangible, than it had earlier been. It was as though the fighting was making the Republic recoil away in horror, making it even harder to reach.

British troops had almost gone from the land, but their influence was still being brought to bear through their guns. Jack's anger began to rise once again at the thought of Collins' men taking orders from British officers and Black and Tans on how to shoot their former comrades. It made him sick to his stomach. Was it these people he was fighting for? He was fighting against them—but also for them. It made no sense. It was as though by shooting a Stater he could finally give him freedom. But what freedom was there in death, in disability? The thought of the Stokes gunner he had shot in the head came back to haunt him. It had just been a target at first, as he was caught up in the whole drama of the battle. Just a green cap sticking out where it shouldn't have been. It had been a simple procedure: Lock and load: Click, click. Aim. Steady, in your sights, slowly squeeze the trigger until the rifle recoils and you see your mark fall. Only it wasn't just a mark. It was an Irishman. A man who had probably fought the Tans as he had done—an Irishman with a mother, a father and sisters and brothers. A man who might have a sweetheart somewhere who was now in mourning, perhaps a wife. Was it now in anger and revenge that he was firing his rifle, where once the feelings were nobler and more idealistic? Was it the drama he was caught up in and not the cause?

'Jack, get your backside up here, they're sending Staters across with petrol bombs. We'll have to get them before they can get close enough to lob them into the buildings,' Barry said, lifting his rifle and taking aim.

Jack jumped to his feet, grabbed his rifle and took up his position at the window in an instant. There was a party of five Staters making their way across the road under the covering fire of a Whippet armoured car, but from the second storey of the Gresham, they were visible.

'Jaysus, that's Mick McGinley,' Thomas said, loading his rifle. He remembered the night in City Hall when McGinley had shown his true colours and the later when they had fought in Conway's pub. 'I knew that bastard was a turncoat—I'll give his mother something to mourn,' he added with a sick grin as he took aim.

Jack froze for a second as a hail of Vickers fire swept the building raising a thick cloud of dust, before he dropped to his knees to take cover. As the firing stopped and the dust began to settle, Jack stood up, took aim and dropped one of the advancing party, whose petrol bomb exploded on contact with the road, setting the dead man alight. Jack quickly turned around when he heard Barry's sobbing begin.

'Ah, Thomas, Thomas,' Barry cried as he cradled his brother's lifeless body on his lap. The back of Thomas' head had been blown off by the exit-wound of a heavy calibre Vickers round. His brains were splattered on the floor beneath him.

Jack raised his rifle once again, saw that McGinley was still advancing, took aim and fired his shot, seeing McGinley spin with the force of the impacting bullet and fall to the ground where he lay motionless, his petrol bomb rolling away towards the curb, unbroken.

'I got him, Barry, I got McGinley for Thomas. I got the bastard,' Jack repeated, reloading his rifle and setting his sights on another target.

'They're retreating,' Seán said. 'Hold your fire.'

Jack let off another round and dropped another soldier, before Seán shouted his order one more time.

'Hold your fire!'

There was a brief lull as the St. John's Ambulance men came out and collected the dead.

Barry was quiet as he sat on the floor, Thomas' body draped across him.

'Get a stretcher up here!' Seán bellowed, sending Frank Hourihan scurrying for stretcher-bearers.

'It's too late,' Barry said, looking up at Seán. 'He's dead.'

Chapter Ten

Less than ten minutes after Thomas had been killed the shelling began in earnest. The eighteen-pounder on Henry Street bombarded every building in turn from the Hibernian Bible Society to Sir James W. Mackey's seed and plant emporium, which lay just beside the Gresham Hotel. The shells were pounding the thin Georgian brickwork into dust and knocking out large chunks, leaving gaping holes in the buildings, through which Free State snipers were doing their best to hit any moving target.

The heavy shelling continued. The number of casualties increased rapidly as floors gave way without the support of outside walls. Confusion was beginning to reign. Everyone knew that it would be just a matter of time before they would have to make a retreat, the bombardment was so heavy.

Thomas's body was taken, along with the many other new fatalities, to a basement room in an adjoining building that was being used as a morgue. In the last three days over twenty volunteers had been killed and fifty wounded by a combination of the recently begun bombardment and sniper fire. Many were inexperienced young men who had only recently joined the IRA in response to the Four Courts attack, whilst one or two were seasoned veterans. Death, it appeared, was not choosy when it came to its victims.

Barry had still not recovered from the death of his brother. He remained in the corner of the hotel room where they were positioned and stared at the bloodstains on the carpet where his brother had fallen. Jack didn't quite know what to do. Barry took a set of rosary beads from his jacket and began praying quietly.

'Jack, Con, I want you two to take up a position in the next room. Frank and I will hold out here for the moment. I'll send Barry into you when he's ready,' Seán said, glancing at Barry, who looked up on hearing his name.

'I'm fine,' Barry said, renewed strength in his voice. 'I'll go with them now,' he added, picking up his rifle and heading out of the room. Jack and Con followed.

Once the barricades had been built up sufficiently they took their positions and began to return fire.

'I'm sorry about Thomas,' Con said, reloading his Lee Enfield, 'he was a good friend and a damned good soldier.'

'Thanks,' Barry replied, turning to Jack. 'I know how you feel too, Jack.'

Jack nodded. He felt a lump in his throat and a tear in the corner of his eye as the rage began, once again, to build up its steam in him. 'They'll pay for it, Barry,' was all that he could say as he began firing at the loopholes in the sandbag emplacements across the street.

The shelling grew more intense as they directed their fire towards the gun emplacements and at the Whippets that patrolled O'Connell Street, raking the buildings with their Vickers guns. The summer sunshine and heat made their attack worse with each hit, leaving every man present covered in dust like ghosts, their bloodshot eyes piercing the dirt with crystal clarity.

'Here they come again,' Con said, seeing another firing party approach the hotel behind a Lancia armoured car, petrol bombs in their hands.

'The Lancia's giving them more protection than the Whippets did, I can't get a clean shot at them,' Jack said, moving from window to window in the hope of finding a fresh mark.

As the armoured car drew closer a shell found its way into the walls of the Gresham, shaking the entire building. It had struck the adjacent room where Seán and Frank Hourihan were positioned.

'I'll check they're all right,' Con said, running through.

Jack took a table and balanced a chair on top of it before climbing up to give himself an extra height advantage. Despite this he was still unable to find a mark amongst the approaching firing party. He had only succeeded in giving the snipers across the street a clear shot at him, which he realised when a bullet tore through the sleeve of his trench coat, missing his arm by less than an inch. He quickly got back into a safer position and began to return fire, aware that the firing party had reached the cover of Mackey's grain store below.

Con returned ashen-faced. 'They got Frank. Seán is fine, but they got Frank,' Con said. 'He wants you to take Frank's place, Jack.'

Jack nodded and went through to the next room.

Frank's body lay in the corner of the room, a huge puncture wound in his chest and blood all over. There was a large hole in the outside wall where the shell had hit and Seán's face was bloodstained from tiny shrapnel and splinter wounds.

'They've got a firing party downstairs. We couldn't get a clean shot at them this time—they used a Lancia to bring them up close. They're throwing petrol bombs in on the ground floor,' Jack said, seeing Seán's furrowed brow.

'We'll hang on here as long as we can,' Seán replied. 'See if you can get any of the firing party whilst I keep the snipers down.'

Seán began firing at the sniper positions across the street

as Jack attempted to get a shot at the firing party through the shell hole. But try as he might, it was impossible. The angle was too sharp. To get a clean shot he would have to literally hang out of the shell hole and fire at the same time, whilst snipers took pot-shots at him.

'It's useless, Seán, I can't get at them,' Jack replied.

'Do we have any grenades?'

'No, not that I know of.'

'Right, I'll be back in a minute,' Seán said, slinging his rifle over his shoulder and leaving the room.

Jack stood alone at his post, feeling true fear for the first time. The broken and bloodied body of Frank Hourihan lay on the floor behind him. Thomas had been killed and Jimmy had been wounded. It felt like it would be just a matter of time before he too was killed. The presence of Frank's lifeless body sent shivers up his spine. Frank, who he had not known until a couple of days earlier, a decent sort, who was full of life, full of fight. And Thomas, poor old Thomas—he had always been an angry man, always ready to use his fists: Dead.

He had always believed that true soldiers felt no fear under fire. That they fought on until the bitter end. It made him painfully aware of how his father must have felt in 1916 when they were surrounded in the GPO with little chance of escape and no chance of success. He had died whilst attempting to help an injured comrade who had fallen from one of the upper windows and whose twisted body lay beside one of the great pillars to the front of the building. In his rescue attempt he was torn asunder by heavy machine gun fire. The same kind of fire that was now moving up along the building as the Whippets drove up and down, stopping when they detected any movement and swinging their turrets around to let loose a hail of death.

Jack's rifle was now shaking in his hands. He held it as tight as he could in an effort to regain control. Fear and rage, anger and pity, it was all there in his mind, mixed up and swirling around uncontrollably. He knew that in order to survive he would need to be hard and strong. It was tearing him apart. His mind, on which he had been relying and which had kept him alive so far, now threatened to be his worst enemy—worse than the Vickers gun, worse than the artillery, worse than the snipers. It was his mind that would get him killed, he thought, dropping a cartridge as he attempted to fill an empty ammo clip.

Seán returned looking tired and anxious.

'We've been told to move down towards the Hammam Hotel—we're regrouping,' Seán said, seeing Jack's rifle shaking in his hands. 'I know how you feel Jack—you're not alone, but we need to keep up our strength. We have to keep fighting for the Republic, for Thomas, for Frank and for Jimmy. We can't give up now,' he said. 'Come on, we'll get the lads and start making a move. The ground floor is already on fire and it's spreading.'

Jack pushed home the ammo clip, checked that his Browning was still under his trench coat and followed Seán into the next room where Con and Barry were still returning fire. He wondered where Helen and Kathy were, and if they were safe. Surely they would be evacuated first, he thought as he collected his gear.

'Come on lads,' Seán said, 'we're going back to the Hammam Hotel. This place is on fire.'

The four men made their way down onto the first floor and from there headed through the holes in the walls to adjoining buildings, passing several dead volunteers on their way, until they reached the Hammam Hotel. The hotel, which was closer to Henry Street than the Gresham, had taken the brunt of the shelling and its Georgian façade had almost collapsed. They were met with over one hundred fellow volunteers and officers who were waiting for Traynor and Brugha to speak.

'There's Dev,' Con said, seeing de Valera's head tower above the men who surrounded him.

'Looks like he's been in the thick of it,' Jack said.

'It wouldn't be the first time,' Seán replied.

Traynor stood up on a table and began to address the men.

'We've held 'the block' as long as we can. So far there has been no sign of reinforcements breaking through as we expected. The last we heard they were stuck up in Blessington in the Wicklow hills. Because of this we've decided to make a tactical retreat. We'll be leaving over the next few hours through the passages and tunnels out towards Marlborough Street and across to Gardiner Street. After that you'll be splitting up into units again. We're back to the old tactics from now on. Cathal Brugha has volunteered to command the rearguard action to cover our retreat. If any of you wants to volunteer for the rearguard then have a word with him. All units from outside Dublin will be heading back to their own areas. We've got to take the war into the country where we are the strongest. Unless there are any questions, I suggest we start moving. Good luck, lads—you fought well,' Traynor said, getting down off the table, shaking Brugha's hand and turning to his adjutant, Paddy Slattery.

'Paddy, get all of our men together. Make sure they're carrying as much in the way of weapons and ammunition as possible—then I want you to talk to the Dublin unit commanders. I have a list of actions drawn up for the next week or so to keep them busy,' he said handing Slattery the list. Slattery looked at the list, smiled, and went on his way.

'So, what do you want to do?' Seán asked, turning to his men.

'I think we should stand and fight,' Barry said with an obvious desire for revenge in his voice.

'How many are staying behind?' Con asked, wondering if it would be a fight to the end.

'There's around twenty men staying to make sure the rest get out safely and to fool the Staters into thinking that we're all still here,' Seán replied.

'I'll do whatever you do,' Jack said, looking at Seán. 'We're still a unit.'

'Right then, we'll stay until they've got most of the men away. I'll have a word with Brugha,' Seán said, walking away.

The sound of gunfire and shelling could still be clearly heard as the three men waited for Seán to return.

Most of the Cumann na mBan nurses were asked to leave first, but a group demanded to stay until the end so that they might look after the volunteers who made up the rearguard action. Jack looked around for Kathy and Helen, but couldn't see them. He silently hoped that they had already left.

Jack's hands were no longer shaking. It was as if he had calmly accepted his fate, whatever it might be. He could feel a strange sense of warmth from within, as though he was being somehow protected, as though he had entered a state of grace. He immediately thought of his father and he knew he was not alone in his time of need.

As the rest of the garrison prepared to leave, Seán returned and led the men through to another building. There, they set up a strong barricade at the windows on the first floor.

'Right, we've got to make it look like there's still a lot of us here—so rapid fire—preferably in the direction of the artillery pieces—but I want one of you to keep the snipers under constant fire too,' Seán said.

'I'll look after the snipers,' Con said, filling the empty ammo clips he had.

'How long do we hold out?' Barry asked.

'Until they rest of them are gone and we're told to leave,' Seán replied.

'Where's Brugha gone?' Jack asked.

'They've headed back over towards the Gresham Hotel. It's important that the Staters see fire coming from along 'the block' so they think we're all still here.'

The men began their rapid firing at the gun emplacements, although there was no real target. The flash and spark of the rounds hitting the armoured cars told them that their aim was true, as the shelling began again in earnest. The Vickers guns poured more lead from their barrels as the two Whippets drove slowly up and down O'Connell Street. It was getting more dangerous by the minute.

It took over an hour for the main body of men to make their way out of 'the block' through the maze of tunnels, lanes and connected buildings. Most made their way out along Gardiner Street, where a few sniper outposts kept the Staters at bay. From there they headed northwards towards Santry and Finglas where there were numerous safe houses where they could find a bed for the night and a meal to restore their strength and will.

By the time the order for the retreat actually came down from the Gresham, it had already fallen. According to the volunteers who were rushing through the buildings, Brugha and a few others had stayed behind to ensure that the rest of the rearguard could make good their escape.

Seán ordered the men to take whatever ammunition they could carry before they headed out towards

Marlborough Street, which they crossed under the protection of friendly snipers. Jack felt the labyrinth of tunnels and passageways close up behind them as they moved onward. They meandered through hotels, public houses, kitchens, private houses and open yards. Jack moved ahead cautiously, making sure that they were clear of Free State snipers before attempting to cross open space. Seán, Con and Barry followed close behind. The men could feel the Staters closing in on them. It was as if every corner, every passage would lead them into the hands of the enemy. Every doorway was a potential ambush point, every wall a blind spot. They moved quickly, carefully.

As they approached Gardiner Street the sound of armoured cars could be heard rattling over the cobble-stones, spitting out heavy calibre bullets at remaining Republican sniper positions. Most of the snipers had already retreated, as they had seen the bulk of the garrison leave 'the block'.

'Looks like we're on our own,' Jack said, turning to Seán as they waited for a chance to make a break across Gardiner Street. An armoured car had just passed them and was making its way up towards Mountjoy Square, so their only hope was to try to make it across to Railway Street, from where they could attempt to head north.

Jack looked across the street. It was only a short walk to his mother's house from here, he thought, suddenly wishing he were there. He knew the area like the back of his hand and that, he thought, might be the one thing that would save them.

'If we head over onto Railway Street we can try to get through the convent gardens. We can head up Rutland Street towards Summerhill—we should be fine from there,' Jack said.

'All right, Jack, this is your patch, you know the alleys.

We'll follow you,' Seán said.

'Right, we need to head straight across here and we should be able to get over the convent gate without too much trouble,' Jack replied, looking up and down Gardiner Street to make sure it was clear. 'Now, let's do it,' he said, making a dash across the road, followed by the others.

On Railway Street the four men stayed to the left-hand side, where the doorways offered some degree of cover. When they reached the convent entrance, which was locked, the men passed their guns through the railings and began to scale the high gate. Seán went first, struggling with his footholds between the narrow railings, followed by Barry and then Con. As Jack began climbing the rumbling sounds of an armoured car filled the air.

'Come on Jack, we've got company,' Seán said.

A Whippet rounded the corner of Buckingham Street and was heading up towards the convent as Jack reached the top of the gate.

'Come on, Jack or they'll see you,' Con said as the three men picked up their guns.

The turret on the armoured car swung to the right as the gunner noticed Jack scaling the gate. The Whippet picked up speed.

As Jack threw his leg over the top of the gate the Vickers gun began to fire, sending the three volunteers on the other side diving for cover behind the gateposts.

Time slowed down in Jack's brain. He could feel every heartbeat, every nerve, every drop of sweat on the palm of his hands as the first bullet struck his leg, shattering a bone. A dull pain crept up his body and made its presence known as the second bullet caught him in the shoulder, throwing him from the gate.

Seán and Barry braved the fire to drag Jack to safety as

Con returned fire, uselessly. The rounds simply bounced off the Whippet as it came closer. Once Jack was under cover, Barry made an attempt to stop the bleeding as Seán raised his revolver and aimed at the viewing slits at the front of the armoured car, through which the driver looked. The Vickers gunner continued to rake the walls of the convent with fire, stopping only when he needed to reload. As the car drew nearer Seán's aim improved as he emptied his revolver at the slit. The car kept coming but then veered off to the right and ran into the convent wall. He had managed to hit the driver.

'Right, let's get Jack out of here,' Seán said, seeing Jack's twisted leg and blood-soaked trench coat.

'His mother's house is only up the road, shall we take him there?' Barry asked, thinking that perhaps Helen and Kathy might be around to tend to his wounds as they had been trained.

'It's too dangerous—he'll be picked up in no time. Any other ideas?' Seán asked.

'Take me up to Jimmy's room on Charles Street. No one will look there,' Jack suggested, feeling the numbness in his wounds give way to a fierce and throbbing pain

'I know where it is, come on,' Con said, picking Jack up by the lapels and throwing him over his shoulder. Although Jack was heavy, Con's strong frame didn't appear to feel the burden.

The four men made their way through the convent garden and over onto Rutland Street, from where it was relatively easy to get to Charles Street through a small alleyway.

'Kick in the door,' Seán said, as they arrived.

Barry put his shoulder to the door and it gave way. The four men entered the building and climbed the stairs.

'Barry, you said Kathy or Helen might have been sent

home from 'the block'—I want you to go and see. Ask them to bring some bandages and food with them,' Seán said.

'Right away,' Barry said, as he lay down his rifle.

'Here, you might need this,' Seán said, handing him his revolver.

Con put Jack on the bed and ripped off the leg of his trousers. It was clear that at least one, if not both of the bones in Jack's lower leg had been broken by the force of the bullet. Removing his coat, Con proceeded to open Jack's shirt to see the extent of the shoulder wound.

'Kathy would be jealous,' Jack said, attempting to joke, his voice punctuated with the pain.

'The shoulder wound doesn't look too bad,' Con said. 'It looks like the bullet went straight through without hitting anything important.'

'You'll be fine, Jack,' Seán said, smiling down at him. 'You'll be fine.'

'What are you going to do now?' Jack asked. He knew that he would be laid up for quite a while.

'I was given orders by Traynor—we have plenty to keep us occupied for a few weeks,' Seán said.

'Will you be staying in Dublin?'

'I don't know. For the time being, anyway.'

'Well, it looks like I'll be here for a while, so if you need a place to stay—you know yourself.'

'This might hurt a bit,' Con said, using a rag torn from Jack's shirt to plug the wound.

'Jesus!' Jack cried. 'There's a dribble of whiskey in a bottle under the bed.'

'Jesus, I never thought I'd see you wanting to waste a drop of whiskey, boy,' Con said with a smile as he searched under the bed. He found a full bottle.

'Just what the doctor ordered,' he said, uncorking it, taking a swig, passing the bottle to Seán and then pouring a little on Jack's wounds. 'Now everyone's happy.'

'I'd be happier if you gave me a drink of it you fucking eejit!' Jack said, gritting his teeth against the pain.

Con handed him the bottle and Jack took a long drink, stopping only when his eyes and throat burned so much that he could no longer take it.

'That's the best anaesthetic you'll find, Jack,' Seán said, as Barry returned with Kathy.

'Oh suffering Jesus what have they done to you?' Kathy asked, bending down to look at Jack's wounds. 'What have they done to you?' She kissed him on the lips, running her fingers through his matted hair and looked him in the eye in an effort to judge how much pain he was in.

'I'll be all right, Kathy, I'll be all right,' Jack said, gritting his teeth as she began examining his wounds.

'I'll look after you, I have everything I need. Don't worry now. I know how to treat gunshot wounds, but we'll have to get a doctor in to look at your leg. I don't really know about setting bones,' she said, as a tear dropped from her cheek. Despite her show of strength and the experience of the last few days in 'the block' she could no longer contain herself. This wasn't just another nameless volunteer—this was her man.

'We'd better be going,' Seán said, looking around at Con and Barry, who didn't quite know what to do.

'Take care lads,' Jack said, as Kathy tended to his wounds. 'I wish I could go with you.'

'I know, Jack. You'll be fighting fit again in a few weeks, don't worry about that. We'll be back for you when you're better,' Seán replied as they made ready to leave.

'Tell Helen that I'm still in one piece, will you?' Barry said to Kathy, 'and that I'll try to get around as soon as it's safe.'

Chapter Eleven

Jack was in agony. Every time he moved a bolt of sharp pain moved up and down his body, forcing him to lie perfectly still while Kathy tended to his wounds.

'Did Barry call straight down to you or did he go to my mother's house?' Jack inquired, wondering if his mother knew of his injuries.

'He came straight to me—I don't think he wanted to face your mother,' Kathy said.

'I can understand that. I haven't met a volunteer yet that my mother couldn't scare,' he said with a forced smile.

Despite her best efforts, Kathy had so far been unable to stem the flow of blood, which slowly soaked through the bandages she applied.

'I'm going to have to go and get a doctor for you, Jack. The bleeding hasn't stopped, and you need to have your leg put in a splint,' Kathy said, kissing his brow. 'I'll drop in on your mother and let her know what happened and where you are.'

'Who are you going to get?' Jack asked.

'Don't worry—Cumann na mBan has a list of sympathetic doctors who'll not say a word. I should have someone here within an hour. And I'll try to get a paraffin heater as well—it's not very warm in this place.'

'Does the leg look bad?'

'It'll take at least two months before it's strong enough to walk on again, I'd say. Your shoulder should be fine in around a month,' Kathy said. 'Now, I'd better be going.

Can I get you anything else before I go?'

'I'm fine, darling, thanks,' Jack said, beginning to feel weak from the loss of blood.

'Less than an hour, I promise, and I'll bring your mother up with me.'

Jack smiled as Kathy put on her jacket and made ready to leave.

'Could you leave that bottle of whiskey where I can reach it,' Jack asked. 'It kills the pain.'

'I'm not sure you should be drinking, but here you are,' she said, leaving the bottle on the bed beside him. 'I'll be back soon,' she added, closing the door.

Jack lay back on the bed and looked around the room. There were water stains on the ceiling and the paint was peeling off. The wallpaper was old and quite grimy and the sash window rattled in its rotten frame as each gust of wind caressed it.

Feeling the pain pulse through his nervous system, Jack opened the whiskey bottle and took another long drink. The moment he was shot flashed through his brain. The whole episode seemed so surreal. Like something you might read in a penny novel or a short story in a newspaper. He was amazed he hadn't been killed. A Vickers gun was capable of spitting out over sixty bullets a minute as far as he knew and the gunner had had a perfectly clear shot at him as he had tried to scale the gate. Only providence had protected him—providence and possibly his father, whose presence he had felt with him since he was in 'the block'.

Unable to keep his eyes open any longer, Jack began falling, falling, falling, until the ever-present pain was but a memory and he was sound asleep. Outside, the city was still in turmoil.

It was summertime and the streets were full of people taking afternoon walks along the quays and up Grafton Street, looking in the shop windows. Everyone was smiling broadly and the blueness of the sky seemed almost unreal it was so deep. As he moved up the street and crossed over into Saint Stephen's Green, he could see children playing ball and young mothers feeding the ducks to the obvious delight of their small children. There was a peaceful presence over the city, as if nothing had happened, as if nothing ever could. The light, the air, the people, the sounds—everything seemed just perfect. He walked around the Green tipping his hat to the ladies he met before stopping at the bandstand to listen to the music. They were playing a melody he had heard before, but which he just couldn't place. He was feeling happy and warm inside, although a little tired. Taking a seat on a bench by the central fountains he watched the children splashing each other, the air filled with their cries of laughter and delight, as nannies patrolled the park pushing perambulators and wiping chocolate-sticky little faces with handkerchiefs. Older gentlemen, their hands clasped behind their backs, strode past with great dignity, all of them looking at him curiously, disdainfully.

A ball rolled to his feet and a small boy came running after it. He picked it up and offered it to the boy, who looked up and into his face. When their eyes met the little boy recoiled in horror. The sound of his scream was unholy. A crowd gathered around him. Gone were the deep blues of the sky, the warmth of the sun, the delight on the faces of the passers-by. All had been replaced by a dark and ominous feeling, a feeling of terror, of death, of destruction. It was as though he had been suddenly transported into a different world, a world of hate, of revenge, of petty hostilities and of bondage.

They began jeering at him and one man stepped forward, punching him in the face, calling him a coward, a blackguard, a killer. There was by now a large crowd gathered in a semi-circle around the bench where he sat. They began to move in closer and closer until he could smell the staleness of their breath, the stench of their sweat. Standing up suddenly, he broke through the crowd and ran out of the Green as fast as he could towards Kildare Street.

The crowd followed him at speed. As he made his way down the street he could see lines of well-dressed men jeering from behind the gates of Leinster House as they flung insults and waved the Union Jack in their efforts to mock him. He looked closer and he could see the gold watch chains of prosperity hanging from their vests, the bellies of butchers hanging over their waistbands, fat rosy cheeks, yet dead, soulless eyes staring blankly, angrily outwards. Men in green uniforms blocked the road up ahead, forcing him to swing left onto Molesworth Street, the crowd growing all the time as he tripped and fell opposite the Masonic Hall. Picking himself up he looked down and saw that he had ripped his trousers and skinned his knees —there was blood running freely down his legs now as he carried on, pursued at every turn by the crowd of people and uniforms.

Down Dawson Street he fled towards Trinity College, where inside its high walls the pampered students were shooting birds in the grounds. Each rifle shot made him tremble as the men in uniform unholstered their weapons and began to fire into the air, shouting at him to stop. He kept running, fear growing with every pace until he fell once more, bloodying his hands. Standing up, he found himself looking at his reflection in a butcher shop window. Inside, carcasses hung by their ankles. Carcasses of men, riddled with bullets, their hearts torn out and placed on trays below for sale to, and for consumption by, the public. His face was drawn—the skin so tight he could almost see his skull, his eyes sunken back in their sockets. Surely this could not be him?

Onward he ran, seeing men with the heads of beasts peering out from shop doorways, their fingers greasy from handling money, their eyes wild with the look of madness. And on Westmoreland Street he saw the bodies of men being poked and prodded by passers-by-men who looked like he did, their bellies torn open, their eyes gouged out, lying limp and hopeless in the gutter while all around laughed and mocked. Onward he ran—the crowd of people and uniforms now coming from all sides as he reached the river.

With his back to the river wall and the crowd growing closer still he blessed himself, sat on the river wall and fell slowly backwards into the dark waters of Anna Livia, whose embrace was warm, much warmer that that of the land. The swirling, eddying motion of the water was almost comforting as it carried him downstream towards and under Butt Bridge until he could no longer keep himself afloat. Under the water he slipped, like a body between freshly laundered sheets, under the water without a breath in his lungs, without a hope for life in his weary mind. Under, under, under.

'It's all right, Jack,' Kathy said, seeing him wake, startled from his dream. 'Dr. Kehoe will see you're all right.'

'Ah Lord God, what have they done to you,' Jack's mother said, looking down at her only son. 'You're going to break my heart, Jack,' she said, wiping a tear from her eye.

'You've been badly hit, Jack,' the doctor said, opening his

bag. He produced a bottle of morphine. 'You must be in great pain.'

' I am,' Jack agreed. 'Can you give me something for it?'

'I'll give you a little shot of this, it should make it easier to deal with. I see you've already been having a little medicine,' the doctor said, seeing the half-empty whiskey bottle.

'It helps,' Jack said, as the doctor gave him the morphine injection and began to undress his wounds.

'You were hit twice? Let me see,' the doctor said, talking to himself as he examined Jack's shoulder, poking around in the entrance wound and turning him over to look at the exit wound. 'Looks like it went clean through you!' he said, almost amazed. 'You're a very lucky man—another inch or two and you could have been dead. It just missed an artery.'

Jack could feel the morphine coursing through his veins ridding his entire body of pain, replacing it with a dull euphoric pleasure that he was beginning to enjoy.

The doctor began his work of closing and dressing the shoulder wound, showing Kathy how to apply the dressing so that it would keep the wound plugged and stop the bleeding, before taking a look at Jack's leg.

'Have you heard what happened after we left O'Connell Street?' Jack asked, looking up at Kathy.

'Brugha was shot. They're not sure if he'll survive,' Kathy said, shaking her head.

'Did he not try to get away?' Jack asked.

'He waited until everyone else was gone and then ran out into the street with his gun in his hand shooting at the Staters. They just cut him down with their machine guns—he didn't stand a chance,' Kathy replied. 'Now, lie back and let the doctor look at your leg, won't you?'

Jack lay back, the pain all the more severe, knowing that

Brugha had been so badly wounded.

'Right,' the doctor said, cleaning the dried blood from the entrance wound, 'let me see.'

Despite the morphine, Jack could feel it as the doctor searched for the bullet in his leg. It wasn't painful, but it felt very strange as the doctor searched for the bullet.

'Right, here we are,' he said, slowly pulling the bullet from his leg and dropping it on a cloth. 'Now all I have to do is set the bone. It looks like it was just the one break, and the bullet seems to have snapped it pretty cleanly—you're lucky it didn't splinter the bone like it usually does,' he said, manipulating the broken bone into place as Kathy handed him a readymade splint. 'You're going to have to stay off this leg for at least a month—so no running around!' the doctor said with a smile.

Jack didn't quite hear him. Everything had become strangely muffled, as though he was wrapped in a big ball of cotton wool. The morphine had begun to take effect.

As Dr. Kehoe closed the leg wound with surgical thread, Helen arrived looking distraught.

'Is he all right?' she asked her mother, who was standing well back, allowing the doctor room to do his work.

'The doctor says he'll be fine—there's no need to worry,' she said, squeezing Helen's arm reassuringly.

'Have you heard anything about Barry,' she asked.

'He's safe,' Jack said, 'but Thomas is dead. He was shot over in the Gresham.'

'Oh merciful hour, oh Lord forgive us,' Jack's mother said aloud, looking up to the heavens. 'That poor boy's mother will be in hell tonight with her grief!'

'How did Barry take it?' Helen asked.

'He's... he's fine,' Jack said, struggling to stay awake.

'I think he could do with a little rest now. He should be left to sleep,' the doctor said, hoping that the small room would empty somewhat.

'I'll look after him, Mrs. Larkin, if you don't mind,' Kathy said. 'The Cumann na mBan training will be useful.'

'I'll go and get some food ready,' Helen said.

'When can we move him home?' Jack's mother inquired.

'I wouldn't do that for a few weeks, Mrs. Larkin, it won't be safe for a while yet. The Staters are rounding up all known Republicans and raiding houses. He'll probably be safer here than anywhere else,' Dr. Kehoe replied, looking down at his patient. Jack had fallen back into a fitful sleep. 'I'll call around tomorrow afternoon and have another look at him. He should be fine, but call me immediately if he breaks out in a fever,' the doctor said, packing his bag and preparing to leave.

'I'll stay with you, Kathy,' Jack's mother said, sitting down by the door. 'Helen, can you bring up that heater we have in the bedroom? He'll need to stay warm,' she added, as Helen too prepared to go home.

Four weeks recovering with his mother and Kathy tending to his needs and Jack was beginning to feel a little better. The shoulder wound had closed up completely and the pain was now but a dull memory. His leg had also healed quite well but would still not take the full weight of his body, forcing him to use a crutch whenever he attempted to move around. They had been the most pleasant weeks of his life, he had told Kathy, thanking her for her care and loving attention. But all the while he was thinking of Seán and the lads out on active service.

Kathy had been filling him in on what the Dublin Brigade had been up to, having heard reports from her Cumann na mBan friends. Most of the bridges in North County Dublin had been blown up in an effort to cut off the capital and stem the flow of troops and equipment that the Staters were using against the IRA around the country. On top of that, a definite campaign of civil disruption was under way, as units attacked and burned government offices in a bid to disrupt the workings of the newly formed State.

But it was in the south that the fighting had really begun to take hold, with battles in Wexford and Waterford resulting in victories on the Republican side. Similar battles were happening all over the country and the Free State government had a difficult time holding the more remote areas as their manpower was stretched to the limit. As it presently stood, Kathy had told him, the IRA were holding the area south of a line from Enniscorthy in Wexford to Limerick in the west, and so far there had been no great opposition. But that was about to change. Plans were already afoot for a full-scale attack on the southern positions held by the IRA as Free State Army recruits continued to pour in.

Jack sat back on the bed as Kathy made a cup of tea with the help of a small Primus stove she had brought from her mother's house.

'I really don't know how Jimmy used to live in these conditions,' Kathy said, shaking her head as she poured milk into the cups.

'I think he used to eat at home most of the time. His Ma did his washing for him too,' Jack said with a smile.

'So why did he want to live here on his own?' Kathy asked, stirring the tea.

'I think he used to use the place to entertain his girl-friends,' Jack said, hoping to shock her.

'Really?' Kathy said, looking around the place with a

fresh pair of eyes, which finally came to rest on the single bed by the window, on which Jack lay.

'Well, that's what he told me—but you know Jimmy—he's all mouth when it comes to the ladies,' Jack said, remembering his old friend.

'Well, he won't be getting many girlfriends visiting him where he is now, up in Mountjoy, will he?'

'Well, at least he's better now,' Jack said.

Kathy had heard from one of her friends that Jimmy had made almost a full recovery. The only remaining evidence of his injury was a scar on his left cheek and the deafness in his left ear.

'So what did he tell you about his girlfriends?' Kathy inquired wondering what Jimmy had got up to in his little love nest.

'Not that much, really,' Jack said with a smile.

'Oh, go on!'

'Well, he said that he had one girl who used to come up here all the time and, well, you know, they used to, to...'

'They never!' Kathy said as she began giggling.

'That's what he said,' Jack replied.

'He's a lucky boy,' Kathy said lifting an eyebrow as the thought of such illicit pleasures filled her mind. She had wanted to be with Jack for the longest time, but there had never been a quiet moment, a place where they could be alone.

'It'll be a while before he gets up to any more mischief,' Jack said with a smile.

'When is your mother coming up?' Kathy asked.

'Around seven this evening, why?'

'I was just wondering, that's all,' Kathy replied, handing Jack his cup of tea and taking a seat beside him.

'I can't wait until this leg heals up. I'm sick of limping around with this crutch,' Jack said, scratching his lower leg with obvious irritation.

'I'll put some fresh bandages on it for you later—they get itchy after a few days. You'll be up and about in no time at all—wait and see—another couple of weeks and you should be able to walk again,' Kathy said, patting him on the knee.

'I don't know what I'd have done without you here to look after me,' Jack said, caressing Kathy's face with his fingers.

'I've enjoyed spending this time alone with you. We've hardly had any time at all together since the war started,' Kathy said, placing her hand on his.

'I love you, Kathy. I've loved you since the first day I laid eyes on you. You're the most beautiful girl I've ever seen,' Jack said, kissing her soft lips.

'I wish this moment could last forever,' she said, as he kissed her once again.

'It will, darling,' Jack replied.

'I can't wait until we're married, Jack,' she said blushing a little.

'I love you more than anything else in this whole world, Kathy.'

He kissed her once again and ran his fingers through her hair.

'Your mother will be here soon,' Kathy said with a smile.

'Of course she will—worse luck,' Jack said, sitting back on the bed with his mug of tea.

Chapter Twelve

The August sunshine beamed through the window. Outside, the shouting of paperboys could be heard as they marched around the streets selling evening papers. Over six weeks had passed since he had been shot and he was back up on his feet, although limping badly. Kathy had returned to her Cumann na mBan activities with Jack's encouragement and she was now to be found in the Suffolk Street offices of Sinn Féin doing administrative work in the afternoons.

Jack sat back on the bed. Over the last few weeks it had become his home. He picked up a book that Helen had brought him from the library. It was an American novel and he was having great trouble maintaining an interest in it. As he began a new chapter, Jack heard someone at the door. It sent him scurrying to his coat in search of his Browning automatic.

'Jack, are you in there?'

'Who's that?' Jack asked, thinking he recognised the voice.

'It's me, Con,' the voice replied.

Jack put the gun into the waistband of his trousers and opened the door. Con stood there, looking a little worse for the wear. His clothes were little more than rags and he looked hungry.

'Jaysus, Con, how are you?' Jack asked, leading his comrade in.

Con sat on the bed.

'Not so bad. Better than I look,' he said with a grin. 'And you?'

'Ah, this fucking leg is taking ages to heal. I'm still limping like peg-leg,' Jack said, shaking his head. 'Another couple of weeks and I'll be back to normal though.'

'Good, we miss you.'

'So, what have you lot been up to?'

'Haven't you heard? We've been all over the feckin' country, boy,' Con said, rolling his eyes to the heavens.

'And?'

'And we've been scaring the shite out of those Free Staters, let me tell you!' he said with a laugh.

'I heard that straight after the fighting in O'Connell Street the brigade went for the bridges in and around the city—is that right?' Jack asked, hoping for confirmation.

'Aye, we got most of them. But the fun only started when we were sent out into Wicklow up into the mountains. Do you remember complaining about the conditions when we were in the Four Courts? Well, you'd be happy enough there now, boy, if you'd been up in them feckin' mountains,' Con said, shivering slightly at the thought of it.

'Cold?'

'You might say that. But we had great fun altogether.'

'Are the lads all right?'

'Barry and Seán? They're fine. They wanted to come over but they had other things to do, and it's not wise to be wandering around Dublin looking like a tramp these days—they're picking up everyone under forty,' Con said, looking down at himself.

'So where are you now? Where are you staying?'

'We've got a spot over by Templeogue. It's handy for the mountains and it's close to the Brigade HQ. We've been doing a lot of courier work recently, shifting messages from one column to another around the country. I've even got my hands on a motorcycle,' Con said with a smile. 'I always wanted one of those yokes.'

'So has the fighting been bad?' Jack asked, anxious to learn the details of the most recent skirmishes so that he could at least live them in his mind.

'Not around Dublin. We've attacked a few spots all right, but the place is crawling with Staters. There's no chance if you don't know what you're doing. We're losing young lads all the time, like, you know.'

'So it's worse down the country?'

'Aye, they've begun to drive us back. And sure when they landed in Cork and outflanked us we knew we'd have to get tough,' Con said, referring to the recent use of ships to transport Free State soldiers to the Republican—held south where they had caught the IRA by surprise. Most units had now fled to the mountains.

'So it's back to hit and run?'

'Back to the old ways. So, how does it feel to be shot by a Vickers gun?' Con asked.

'It's fucking sore, I wouldn't recommend it,' Jack replied with a smile.

'Has the shoulder healed up?'

'Yeah, it's fine now,' Jack said thinking how uncomfortable it still was to sleep on his left side. 'Here's the bullet the doctor took out of my leg,' he said, pulling the piece of dented lead from his pocket.

'Jaysus, it's big enough. You wouldn't want to catch one of those in the head,' Con said, suddenly remembering that Thomas had done exactly that.

'How's Barry?' Jack asked.

'Ah, he's all right. We all are. It's not easy, but sure we have to keep going,' Con said, cleaning the dirt from under his fingernails.

'Do you fancy going for a pint?' Jack asked, wondering if he could limp as far as the local pub on Gardiner Street.

'Can you manage?'

'As long as I've got the crutch, no problem,' Jack said, looking forward to getting out of the room for the first time since being shot.

'Maybe I should have a quick splash and get some of this muck off me,' Con said. 'And sure we could drive down to the pub on the motorcycle—it'll save you limping.'

'Great idea—there's a bucket of water over there by the door,' Jack said. 'And I've got a clean shirt you can have.'

Once Con had cleaned himself up a little the two made their way downstairs. Jack got on the back of the motorcycle, the crutch under his arm, and Con sped off down the street.

'We may as well go somewhere we can get a decent pint, seeing as we have the bike,' Jack shouted above the noise of the engine, feeling the fresh wind rushing through his hair. It was heaven after all of those weeks cooped up in Jimmy's room.

'Any suggestions?'

'Mulligan's?'

'No problem.'

Mulligan's was quiet, with only five or six men sitting at the bar, but there was a definite feeling of tension in the air. Jack and Con took a table in the bar by the window and ordered two pints of porter. A paperboy entered, selling copies of *The Evening Herald.* Jack bought a copy.

'Jaysus, Griffith is dead,' Jack said, almost disbelieving the news as he read the headline.

'Well, we didn't shoot him,' Con said quickly, sure that he'd know by now if they had.

'It says here he had a brain haemorrhage this morning.'

'Do you think it'll change things—the way Collins is behaving?'

'What, the way he's been selling us out? Do you think it was all down to Griffith?' Jack asked.

'Well, he was one of the big shots,' Con said.

'I don't think it'll change a thing,' Jack said, paying the barman as he delivered the two pints of porter.

'Well, here's to getting you back to the firing line,' Con said, lifting his glass.

'Sláinte!'

Jack was beginning to feel what he considered normal again. Con had always been a good man to have a drink with. He was always well informed and usually had some good stories and jokes to tell.

'Have you heard the latest from Mountjoy?' Con asked.

'Go on.'

'The guards there shot two of our lads dead during an escape attempt three days ago. And a few others have died as a result of ill-treatment in the last month as well.'

'Isn't there any way we can put a stop to it?'

'We could take a few pot-shots at the Governor, I suppose, but I think it might just make things harder for the lads.'

The two men sat and talked for over three hours before Con dropped Jack off at Jimmy's room on Charles Street. Jack felt a little worse for the wear. Promising to come and collect him in a couple of weeks, Con got on his motorcycle and made his way onto Mountjoy Square from where it was a straight run down to the quays.

Jack hopped up the stairs and found himself back in the confines of the small room. He closed the door and made straight for the bed, feeling the porter flow through his veins. He lay back on the bed and quickly fell asleep.

Kathy arrived at around six o'clock that evening only to find Jack snoring drunkenly. Wondering where he had got the drink, as the whiskey was long gone, she sat on the bed and put her hand on his face. Jack slowly began to wake up, opened his eyes, and saw Kathy on the bed beside him.

'Are you feeling all right?' she asked.

'I'm fine. Con called around a few hours ago and we went out for a drink. He had a motorcycle with him,' Jack said, hoping that would explain his movements.

'You've been out drinking?'

'Just a couple over in Mulligan's. He said he'd come to collect me when I'm up and running again,' Jack said, looking forward to the day.

'It'll be a few weeks yet,' Kathy said, shaking her head and wishing the day would never come. If she had her way, she thought, he'd be locked up in the room until the war was over.

'Have you heard about Griffith,' Jack asked.

'Yes, I heard it this afternoon. Terrible, isn't it? Do you think it might bring people back to their senses?'

'Not at all. It'd take the death of someone much more influential to change anything.'

'What, like Collins?'

'Maybe. But even then I don't know if it would change anything. They've been going too far recently, what with killing prisoners and shooting volunteers on sight—they can't expect to get away with that sort of behaviour. No one wants to fight, but they're giving us no choice.'

'I know. I just hope that someone can put an end to it,' Kathy said, stroking his face with her hand.

The weeks spent recovering from his wounds had renewed his belief that what the Free Staters were doing was morally and politically wrong. It was, he reasoned, up to men like him to see that it didn't continue.

'His funeral is in a day or two. I'd say it'll be a big affair,' Kathy said. 'They'll probably shut the entire city centre down for the day. Would you like to go down to it if you're feeling strong enough?'

'Yeah. I'd like to see what O'Connell Street looks like from the outside these days—I haven't seen how much damage they did—it's hard to tell when you're on the inside, though I'd imagine that half of the buildings are in ruins by now.'

'The whole eastern side of the street is in bits—but they've cleared all of the rubble away and are starting to repair it,' Kathy said.

'Well, let's hope they put in thicker walls for the next time,' he said with a smile. 'Those Georgian buildings can't stand a heavy pounding.'

'I think it's over for now,' Kathy said, 'and the open fighting in the south looks like it's coming to an end too. Most of the units have fled into the mountains, according to the girls down in Suffolk Street. They say that the fighting is going to get dirtier by the day.'

'That's what they want from us. That's what they're forcing us to do and that's what they'll get. The Flying Columns will make their mark again, let me tell you,' Jack said, thinking how hard life would be for the men in the mountains.

Jack was back up on his feet again and had rejoined Con, Barry and Seán in their new outpost beyond Ballsbridge. Much had changed in the past few months.

Following Griffith's death in the early days of August, Michael Collins was shot dead in County Cork on his way, some said, to a meeting with de Valera in an effort to reach some degree of a settlement. From then on things had begun to get worse.

The men had grown more bitter as atrocities were carried out on both sides, with many men acting on their own behalf and not on orders. Republican positions in the south had fallen and most units were now operating solely on a hit and run basis, retreating to the mountains to regroup and plan further attacks. Free State troops now held most of the towns and villages around the country. In some areas the fighting had come to a standstill and the lack of effective Republican leadership was to blame. The fighting in Kerry had become particularly savage with several unforgivable atrocities hardening the resolve of the opposing factions.

Ernie O'Malley, who had escaped from the Distillery after the fall of the Four Courts and who had spent the rest of the summer fighting in the south, had returned to Dublin as the Assistant Chief of Staff of the IRA. He was intent on making as much of an impact on the Free State forces stationed in the capital as possible.

In an effort to reduce the number of Republican soldiers, the Free State government had offered a short amnesty to all those willing to dump their arms and undertake a commitment to refrain from rejoining the war. A move that was made in tandem with the amnesty offer was the introduction of the Special Powers Act and the setting up of military courts. The Special Powers Act laid out a list of offences that could be punished by death, penal servitude and deportation. Everything from taking part in an attack on Free State forces to looting, arson or the possession of arms or explosives was punishable by the death penalty. Despite the introduction of the Special Powers Act, however, nobody believed that the government would really begin executing Republicans.

Barry had been wounded in late August while on active

service in the Dublin Mountains. A ricochet had embedded itself in his forearm while he was attacking a Free State patrol south of Blessington. He had taken to showing the scar at every possible opportunity. It was, Jack felt, as if Barry were trying to prove that he had been shot, but that he had been lucky enough to survive, unlike his brother Thomas. Jack thought the way he showed the scar to the young recruits was unhealthy. Con, on the other hand, had forgotten all about the wound he had sustained in the Four Courts until Jack reminded him. Barry obviously felt guilty about being alive, Jack thought, remembering how he had cradled Thomas' body in his arms after he had been shot dead.

The unit spent the early weeks of October acting as couriers between command posts in the city, a job which was getting increasingly dangerous owing to the large number of Free State patrols. But they were itching for some real action. They didn't have to wait long.

Seán had a long meeting with O'Malley, who had been having discussions with a high ranking Catholic Monsignor from the Irish College in Rome. The Monsignor was also holding talks with Richard Mulcahy, Minister for Defence with the pro-Treaty government, in the hope of stopping the fighting, or at least scaling it down. O'Malley had asked the Monsignor to pass on a message to Mulcahy, requesting that the actions of the CID based in Oriel House, on Westland Row, be curbed. The murder gangs, as they had become known, were groups of CID men who were particularly brutal in their treatment of Republicans. Torture and summary execution on the streets were becoming their speciality and their actions were creating a lot of bitterness in the process.

But as no reduction in the activities of the Oriel House CID squads was made, O'Malley had begun to plan an attack on the building to exact some degree of revenge for their indiscriminate and brutal methods.

The plan was to storm the building and to take as much of their paperwork as was possible. As they had been the most active and destructive CID unit in Dublin, their files, O'Malley believed, would give the IRA a better idea of what they were up against. At the same time the CID arsenal would easily re-arm a battalion, and arms had become scarce in the capital.

Once Seán had been given the details of the proposed raid he called the volunteers around to give them their orders.

'We're going to attack and take Oriel House tonight, men,' Seán said, seeing the men's faces change from looks of expectation to looks of concern. 'We'll be going in just after teatime, so they should be off their guard. The plan is to take the entire building, steal as many of their documents as possible for intelligence purposes and make a tactical retreat as soon as possible.'

'So we're just going after their papers?' Jack asked.

'And their guns—they have an arsenal in there that will be very useful to the lads in the Third Battalion. I hear they have over fifty rifles and small arms. We've been losing a lot of guns recently, what with the raids they're making on our arms dumps and informers giving them up. Apart from all that though, it'll give you a chance to take a few shots at those vicious bastards. They've caused a lot of trouble for us in the past few months, and it's high time they paid the price for it,' Seán said, matter-of-factly.

'So, how are we supposed to do it?' Barry asked, looking unsure.

'We're going in via Merrion Square, while some of the

Third Battalion will be coming up from Lombard Street at the same time. Two or three of you will approach the door, ask for an off-duty officer and when they open the door you hold them up while the rest of us enter. It should be a piece of cake—we'll be going in just after they've had their dinner, so they won't be expecting anything,' Seán said with a smile.

'Jaysus, they'll get a great kick out of this,' Jack said, looking at Con, who nodded unsurely, raising his eyebrows as he did.

'We'll be posting snipers all along the rooftops in the area once we have the building under control so we can keep the streets clear of troops,' Seán added.

'How long will we be in there?' Con asked.

'We'll go in and out as quickly as possible. There's no point in sitting and waiting for them to blow us out of it again, is there?' Seán replied.

Jack was worried. Since he had gone back on active service all he had been doing was courier work, and while that was dangerous enough these days it was nothing at all in comparison to what Seán was planning. Oriel House was sure to be well protected and well fortified. On top of that there was a definite lack of escape routes in the immediate vicinity. Oriel House was located on the lower corner of Westland Row. The only way out, in Jack's opinion, was down Lombard Street and away onto the quays, from where it might be possible to get to the other side of the city, or to head out towards Sandymount. The Merrion Square side, with its many government buildings, was sure to be a hive of activity, no matter what the time of day was.

Seán had been given plans of the building by O'Malley, who had met an informer and had gone over the drawings with him. As a result, they knew exactly what they were up against. The plan laid out specific goals for each participating volunteer. One would go to the first floor in search of their files, while another would take control of the armoury. That way, O'Malley had explained to Seán, everything would get done much faster and with greater efficiency.

'We're going in at eight-thirty, lads, so you'd better get yourselves together,' Seán said, looking at his watch. 'It's six-thirty now.'

Jack, Con and Barry were to be the advance party who would break their way into the hallway, followed swiftly by the boys of the Third Battalion. Once inside they were to ensure that each floor was held, secure the telephones, raid for documents and gather together any arms and ammunition that could be found. It sounded easy enough when explained in such a manner, but with upwards of twenty armed men on the other side of the door they were going to storm it was going to be anything but easy.

Barry went out to the back garden of the house they were staying in and sat on a low wall that encircled a raised flowerbed. Jack went out and sat down beside him.

'All right?' Jack asked.

'I don't know, Jack. I just don't know anymore,' Barry replied.

'We'll be fine. It's a piece of cake.'

'I felt quite numb after Thomas was killed and it helped me to carry on. But that numbness is gone and what I'm left with is fear. I'm scared, Jack. For the first time in my life I'm truly scared. This feels like it's going to be the last thing I ever do. It's as though I've had a premonition of my death. I can't do it, Jack, I just can't do it anymore.'

'Look, me and Con will go in before you, so you won't be in the line of fire—how does that sound?' Jack asked.

'Thanks, you're a good friend, Jack, but it's not that. It's the whole bloody war. I'm weary of it. The amnesty has come to an end and here we are running around with guns in our hands—they'll have us up against a wall over in Portobello Barracks in no time, filling us with bullets and throwing us into quicklime graves. I thought it would all be over by now, that someone would bring an end to this mess we've created, that maybe Liam Lynch would see that we were being broken down. There's no discipline amongst the ranks anymore. No one knows what anyone else is doing and attacks aren't being made around the country to achieve anything. It's turned into a street fight, not a war about the Republic. It's over, Jack. At least for me.'

'You can't leave us now, Barry. What about fighting for Thomas? They killed him. He died fighting for the Republic. If you give in now then his death will have been in vain,' Jack said, standing up.

Barry got swiftly to his feet and threw a punch at Jack, knocking him to the ground.

'Don't you talk about my brother—I'll break your fucking neck, do you hear me?' Barry shouted, attracting the attention of Con and Seán who were standing just inside the back door.

'Go on then,' Jack said, rubbing his jaw. 'Turn tail and run. Don't you understand that we've been facing death since we started all of this? All along the way we've been shot at, bombed, beaten and imprisoned. But we're still going. They can't defeat us, Barry. Not if we stay strong,' Jack said, getting back on his feet.

'My family have always been strong Republicans. We've always done our bit and we've lost enough men. I'm not going to join them. I want to live, God damn it! I don't want to rot away in a grave, a footnote in a history book. I want to live.'

'You don't get it, do you?' Jack said, shaking his head. 'We are history. We are the ones who will shape the future of this country by what we do now. If we stop now we've failed—every single volunteer who has died, every patriot who has given his life in the cause of Ireland's freedom will have died in vain. We are on the verge of achieving what they never could and you want to throw it all away?'

'There's been too much killing. Brothers are fighting brothers—fathers are fighting their sons. It's tearing the country apart and I won't be a part of it anymore,' Barry said, walking towards the house. 'We've lost, they've won, can't you see it?'

'Thomas was a better man than you'll ever be,' Jack said with venom. 'He wouldn't give in.'

Barry turned, looked Jack in the eye and then turned away, heading back into the house.

Con came out to see what all of the fuss was about as Barry spoke with Seán.

'What's wrong with Barry?' Con asked.

'He's packing it in. He doesn't want to fight anymore—says he's had enough.'

'Are you serious?' Con asked, not believing what he had just heard. Barry had been one of the strongest willed, most fearless fighters in their unit and had never lost his nerve under fire. He was no coward: that was for sure. So why would he suddenly give up the fight? Con just didn't understand. 'What reason did he give?'

'He just said he's had enough of the fighting and killing—he says we've lost the war already but we don't know it.'

'Jesus, Mary and Joseph. I never thought I'd hear Barry say anything like that. Are you sure?'

'I'm as sure as I'll ever be. Hasn't he just gone to have a

word with Seán?'

'He has.'

'Well, I think we won't be seeing Barry again. He's finished.'

'But Seán wouldn't let him leave now. It might compro-
mise the raid on Oriel House.'

'That's true. He'll probably leave him here under guard
until we've come back,' Jack said, wondering if that was
what Seán would insist on.

Seán came out into the back garden.

'You know that Barry's not coming with us tonight
then?' Seán asked.

'Or any other night,' Jack replied. 'He's out, isn't he?'

'I'm sad to say he is, yes.'

'So, what are you going to do about the raid tonight?'
Con asked.

'I'll take Barry's place. He'll be staying here until we get
back. I'm leaving one or two lads to make sure he stays
here until we've finished up at Oriel House.'

'You don't think that he'd give the game away, do you?'
Con asked.

'No, I don't, but he's a very angry man right now, so it's
better for him that he stays here, just in case something
does go wrong and we think it was him,' Seán said. 'It's
better this way and he understands why I want him to
hang on for a while longer. You'd best start getting ready.
We leave in twenty minutes.'

Jack and Con went back into the house to get their guns
and ammunition. As they made their way towards the
stairs Jack saw Barry sitting in the front room, his head in
his hands, as another volunteer stood at the front door
with his rifle, guarding the entrance. It was as if Barry
were suddenly the enemy—no longer trustworthy. He
had fought and fought well all through the Tan War and

in the war against the Staters until today, yet here he was under armed guard, five minutes after deciding he wanted to give up. It seemed surreal, Jack thought, still angry with his friend for giving up on the fight. But it wasn't Barry that Jack was angry with—it was himself. He understood completely why Barry felt as he did and if the truth were to be known he too was afraid. It was as if the others had kept him strong all the way through the conflict, that seeing them made him believe he was good enough, strong enough, and that he had enough fight to carry him through to the end, whatever that might be. But to see Barry leave under such circumstances chipped away at Jack's own ideological foundations and it vexed him greatly. Everything that Barry had said swirled around in Jack's head as he loaded his Browning automatic and gave it a quick rub with an oily rag. When he was finished the gun shone like a new weapon.

'Come on,' the shout came from downstairs. 'We're ready to go.'

With that, Jack and Con made their way downstairs and joined Seán and four others outside the house. They began their walk into the city centre, breaking up into groups of two. They travelled on opposite sides of the road, their weapons hidden under their trench coats.

The dark evening was lit only by the gaslights on Pembroke Road as the fallen leaves, whipped up in the wind, blew around the streets. It was cold and the streets were quiet as the people of Dublin sat down for their dinners, just like the CID men in Oriel House would be doing, Jack thought, feeling the weight of the Browning under his belt.

As the party of men made their way across Merrion Square, Jack, Con and Seán to the fore, all was quiet. O'Malley, who had insisted on coming along on the operation, took up the rear with a couple of divisional officers.

The unit moved onto Merrion Street Lower and across Lincoln Place onto Westland Row, from where they would make their way northwards towards Oriel House. If all went according to plan, they would see the men of the Third Battalion on Lombard Street, waiting for the signal to go in.

Jack looked behind him to check where O'Malley and the rearguard were. There was no sign of them. On Seán's orders they continued on their path until they were across the street from the CID building. A group of five men were making their way towards Oriel House from Lombard Street. As Seán gave the order to advance on the position, Con spotted an armoured car turning onto Westland Row from the southern end.

'They must be the lads from the Third battalion,' Seán said, seeing the men cross over onto Westland Row. He was wrong. It was a group of railway workers on their way home from work.

'There's a Whippet up the street,' Con said, excitedly.

'Never mind—we're going in now,' Seán said, removing his revolver from beneath his coat and heading across the road, Jack and Con on his heels.

Seán knocked on the heavy door of Oriel House and the door opened slightly, on a chain, and a man peered out at them.

'What is it?' the man said in a rather gruff voice.

Seán brought the revolver up to the man's face as Jack and Con forced the door open. Inside, four men stood at the reception desk whilst three more were climbing the stairs. In the ensuing confusion one of the men behind the desk withdrew his short arm and took aim at Seán as he struggled with the man on the door. Jack brought the Browning out from under his coat and fired four times, hitting the man behind the desk at least twice, while Con took aim and shot one of the men on the stairs. Seán's revolver went off and the men he was grappling with fell to the floor.

'There's no back up, let's get out of here,' Seán said, firing at the men on the stairs as they retreated. The three men ran toward Lombard Street as the Whippet came ever closer.

The uninjured CID men drew their weapons and followed the three volunteers out onto the street. Jack turned, raised the Browning and pulled the trigger, seeing the CID men run back inside the building in search of cover. Once they no longer posed an immediate danger, he ran up the road after Con and Seán who were providing covering fire for him.

A detective returned fire with a rifle from the first floor window of Oriel House. Jack could hear the bullets zing past his head as he ran. The cobblestones shattered ahead of him as the rounds hit the road. It was too close for comfort.

'Run for it,' Con screamed as they heard the sound of small arms fire from Oriel House.

The three men ran down Lombard Street, onto Townsend Street and ducked into a garden on Princes Street South before making their way over Butt Bridge. From there they headed north up Amiens' Street. They had succeeded in losing the detectives, and there was no sign of the armoured car.

'Let's go up to Jimmy's place on Charles Street. We can stay there until the fuss dies down,' Jack said, breathless from the running. He was still unfit following his leg wound, which had begun to ache anew under the present strain. Once they had safely reached Jimmy's room they began to question what had gone wrong.

It was understandable, Jack said, that O'Malley and the rearguard were stopped in their tracks as the armoured car had appeared from nowhere, but there was no reason why the Third Battalion should fail to turn up—unless they too had run into difficulties. One thing was for sure though—the raid was an unmitigated disaster.

'At least we managed to plug a few CID men,' Con said, in an effort to cheer them up.

'But we don't know what happened to O'Malley and the others,' Seán said. 'They could've been captured for all we know.'

Later that night Seán, Jack and Con made their way back across the city using the lanes and side streets that had become their normal routes. As they approached their outpost in Ballsbridge, Seán noticed several men standing around trying to look relaxed, smoking cigarettes and walking up and down the street.

'They've raided the house,' Seán said. 'Let's get out of here.'

'If they raided the house, then they would've got Barry and the other fellow that you left to guard him,' Con said to Seán.

'Barry should've come with us,' Jack said, shaking his head.

'Well, he didn't,' Seán said, unsympathetically.

Two days later they learned that one of the rearguard party had been stopped on Mount Street Bridge by a group of CID men, wounded, and then shot dead at close range. It was starting to get rough.

Chapter Thirteen

October 1922

Much had happened since the raid on Oriel House. It had been established that Barry had been taken prisoner along with the volunteer who had been left behind to guard him. Both were now to be found in Mountjoy Gaol, waiting for their trial under the special military courts.

It appeared that Barry had been given a pistol by the volunteer guarding him once the house had been surrounded. The two men attempted to fend off the raiding party and make good their escape. It was not to be. After less than twenty minutes both men were out of ammunition and were captured.

Jack, Con and Seán were busy. Ernie O'Malley was in the process of arranging safe houses across the city for Liam Lynch, Eamon de Valera and Erskine Childers, so that the newly formed Provisional Republican Government could begin to operate and make its presence known. In doing this he had sent Jack and Con out in search of suitable lodgings. Seán began organising an increase in attacks around Dublin—a role more fitting his rank as one of the top men in the Dublin Brigade.

Things were happening quickly in the early days of November. With so much traffic coming and going from the new Dublin HQ its whereabouts was becoming common knowledge. This led to the capture of Ernie O'Malley on the fourth, following a lengthy shoot-out in which he was riddled with bullets. He was taken to Portobello

Barracks Hospital where he almost died.

With the fall of the Dublin HQ much of the IRA's organisational paperwork was lost. It was a serious blow. Nevertheless, Con, Jack and Seán continued to search for suitable accommodation for the Republican leaders who were due to arrive in the capital.

On the tenth of November another serious blow saw Erskine Childers arrested. In one of life's great ironies, the pistol that brought about Childers' arrest, had been given to him only a year before by Michael Collins. Childers was the movement's Director of Publicity and had orchestrated an effective campaign of information distribution with his newspaper, *An Phoblacht* and other publications. As he was caught in possession of a pistol, Childers would face trial by the new and secretive military courts operating under the Special Powers Act.

On the day of Childers' trial, the seventeenth of November, four volunteers who had recently been arrested in possession of firearms were executed. Barry was amongst their number.

Upon hearing of Barry's execution, Jack withdrew into himself for a number of days, seeing the injustice of what the Staters had done. He knew that they must be made to pay for what they were now doing. Several days after Barry's execution by firing squad in Beggar's Bush Barracks, Erskine Childers was executed. The remaining Republican leadership began making plans for reprisal attacks.

Seán's countenance had changed in the days following the executions and there was little spoken of other than the desire for revenge. Once Liam Lynch's orders had been received, surveillance operations were undertaken around the city in an effort to locate government ministers and officials who supported the Special Powers Act. The plan was to burn their homes and property and perhaps wound them, in an effort to let the acting government know that the IRA was serious about their threat of reprisal shootings. Seán had instructed Con and Jack to gather intelligence on a number of people. Other units across the city were doing the same thing.

Two days later Jack heard that Sean Hales, one of the government ministers who had supported the introduction of the Special Powers Act, had been shot dead by IRA volunteers. Another minister, Pádraig Ó Máille, had been seriously wounded. The response from the Free State government was swift and brutal. The following morning Liam Mellows, Rory O'Connor, Dick Barrett and Joe McKelvey were woken in their prison cells, taken out into the prison yard and shot to death as an act of retaliation. They had not been tried under the Special Powers Act and had been captured before the general amnesty had ended. It was State-sanctioned murder.

Jack, Con and Seán were going over the intelligence notes that they had been compiling at a temporary HQ when a volunteer arrived with news of the executions. Jack wept openly when he heard the news, his tears quickly turning to anger.

'Just tell me who you want me to plug, Seán. Just tell me. We can't let them get away with it,' he said, fighting back the tears.'

'Don't worry, Jack,' Seán said, his eyes dull with a desire for revenge. 'We'll make them pay for what they did.'

'Give me a name, any name. I'll go out and do it now,' Jack replied, reaching for the Browning under his coat.

'I'm with you, boy,' Con said echoing Jack's thoughts.

Seán left the room in silence. Jack paced back and forth

until he was fit to explode.

'If they want to play dirty, then we'll give them what they're after,' he said, staring down as his gun. It was as if a switch had been flicked in his soul. Gone were the lofty ideals which had brought him into the fold of the Republican Movement, all that remained was the desire for revenge; revenge for the death of his comrades, revenge for the murder of Liam Mellows, his inspiration and role model.

'We'll make them pay, don't you worry,' Con said, slumping down in a chair as though the wind had been knocked from him.

Chapter Fourteen

The following morning Seán called Jack and Con together. If they were going to act in response to the murders,
they would have to act quickly, he told them. Pulling a list
of names from his jacket pocket, Seán scanned it slowly,
wondering whom he would pick. The list contained
twelve names. Some were government ministers, some
were civil servants and some were Free State officers. The
ministers would be hard targets just now, following the
Hales killing. The civil servants, he thought, while responsible for much of the paperwork that ran the government,
could not be held directly responsible for the actions of
the government and its ministers. Free State officers, on
the other hand, were a law unto themselves at times. Seán
read officers' names. He knew two of the four names on
the list. They had served with him during the Tan Fight.
The other two names meant nothing to him. One of them,
he had been told, had been involved in putting firing parties together for the first executions—when Barry had
been shot in Beggar's Bush Barracks. He had made his
decision. The officer's name was McCormick.

'The man you're targeting is called McCormick,' Seán
said slowly. 'We believe he put the firing party together
for the first executions, which as you know, included
Barry.'

'Don't you want us to get a minister?' Jack asked, thinking that they only thing the government would under-

stand was the death of one of their own.

'It's too risky right now. They'll all have armed guards with them from now on. It would be a suicide mission, and I'll not have you throwing your lives away on some gob-shite government minister,' Seán replied.

'Where can we find him,' Con asked. McCormick was not one of the people that they had been following in recent days and they had never heard of him before today.

'He's living with his mother on Fitzwilliam Square. I want this done tomorrow, Saturday. We have no details of what he does when he's off-duty,' Seán said, handing Jack a slip of paper with McCormick's address and description on it.

'I want you to kill him,' he said, buttoning up his coat and leaving the house.

'What do you think?' Jack asked, sitting down on the bed.

'I think I need a drink,' Con said.

'It's about time they had a taste of their own medicine,' Jack replied, staring over to where his Browning pistol lay on a chest of drawers.

'To Barry,' Con said, uncorking a bottle of whiskey and taking a swig.

'To all our fallen comrades,' Jack said, taking the bottle from Con. He drank deeply.

'Where do you think we should do it?' Con asked.

'Somewhere crowded. That way we'll be able to get away without any trouble.'

'That could be difficult.'

'The town will be full of people out shopping tomorrow, so we'll be able to melt into the crowd and get away,' Jack said, suddenly remembering the strange dream he'd had whilst convalescing.

'If we rode up beside him on a motorcycle we could get

a shot at him without any problem and then just drive away,' Con said, thinking that it would make their escape somewhat easier.

'Right so, we'll use a motorcycle. It'll give us a better chance of getting away,' Jack said, returning his gaze to the Browning.

Jack and Con rose early on Saturday morning, cleaned their guns and went to pick up the motorcycle they intended to use. The bike belonged to a friend of Con's who, although a Republican, had never seen fit to fight for his beliefs.

Making their way up along the North Circular Road the two volunteers turned right onto Synott Row and made their way onto Inisfallen Parade, where Mick Sheehan lived with his mother. It was a small terraced house with a battered front door. Jack knocked loudly.

A voice came on the other side of the door.

'Who's that?'

'It's me, Con.'

'Just a minute,' the voice replied, unlocking the door and opening it wide. 'How are you Con? And it's Jack, isn't it?'

Jack nodded, smelling the stale stench of porter off Mick's breath. He looked like he had just got out of bed.

'Listen, Mick, I need the bike for a few hours, is that alright with you?' Con asked.

'As long as you have it back in one piece, I don't mind. Where are you off to?' he asked.

'Ah, it's business. You know yourself,' Con said, knowing that he would ask no further questions.

'You might need to put a sup of petrol in her. I was going to last night on the way home from work, but I forgot all about it,' Mick said, shaking his head. 'I'm surprised I actually remembered to come at all last night, I was so drunk,' he said with a smile.

'Where is it?' Con asked, anxious to get down to business.

'Ah, she's out the back. You'll have to come through the house,' Mick said, gesturing that they should go through to the back yard.

The house was warm. The smell of turf smoke wafted out from the kitchen as they made their way through to the back door. Jack could see an old woman sitting by the fire, drinking a cup of tea. She looked up as the men entered the kitchen.

'How are you Mrs. Sheehan?' Con asked.

Jack nodded in her direction.

'I'm fine, Con. And yourself?'

'Ah, dragging the divil be the tail,' Con replied with a smile, opening the back door and going out into the yard.

'Con's just going to borrow the bike for a few hours, Mam,' Mick said by way of an explanation.

'Close out that door, son, or I'll die the death of cold,' Mrs. Sheehan said as Mick joined the two volunteers in the yard.

'Here she is,' Mick said, pulling back the canvas sheet that kept the rain off the bike. 'Be sure an' take good care of her now, won't you?'

'I will, Mick. I'll have her back for you this afternoon, all right?'

'Just go easy on her. The chain's a bit loose. I've been meaning to tighten her up, but sure, you know yourself,' Mick said.

Con started the bike while Mick opened up the back gate onto the lane. Jack got on the back. Within minutes they were speeding up the North Circular Road towards Phibsborough, where they turned left onto Constitution Hill and headed down towards the river by the Four

Courts. They crossed Whitworth Bridge and made their way to St. Stephen's Green, from where they headed over to Fitzwilliam Square, where McCormick lived with his mother.

Con pulled over to the side of the road and Jack dismounted, looking up and down the street for Civic Guards or Staters. Once they knew that the coast was clear, the two men left the bike and made their way into the square, finding a bench that afforded a good view of McCormick's house.

'We'll be able to spot him from here when he makes a move,' Jack said.

'Where do you think we should do it?' Con asked.

'Let's just follow him and see where he goes.'

Fitzwilliam Square was relatively quiet, with only one or two nannies pushing prams and guiding toddlers through the greenery. It was a nice morning, fresh, as though it might rain, but bright enough to suggest that the sun might eventually show its face through a break in the grey clouds.

Sitting quietly, the two volunteers kept an eye on McCormick's front door as a jarvey pulled up outside, climbed the eight steps and knocked loudly with the end of his walking stick on the big blue door. A moment later McCormick emerged buttoning up his tunic. He followed the jarvey down the steps toward the sidecar. The horse whinnied nervously, scraped his hoof on the cobblestones and raised his head impatiently.

McCormick climbed up on the sidecar, secured his hat and spoke to the jarvey.

Jack nudged Con lightly, a dark look in his eyes.

'Let's get going. We don't want him to get away from us now, do we?'

'Right,' Con replied, straightening his trench coat.

The two men made their way out of the square to the motorcycle and started it up, giving the jarvey a lead of a few hundred feet.

The sidecar made its way up onto Leeson Street Lower and turned towards St. Stephen's Green. The horse began biting at the bit as the jarvey tapped his rear-end with a whip.

'Easy there boy,' the jarvey said, loosening the reins a little, hoping that the horse would quieten down.

McCormick sat there with a grim look on his face as they made their way around the Green towards Grafton Street.

Con applied a little throttle and the motorcycle caught up with the sidecar. Jack removed the Browning from beneath his jacket with one hand, while pulling down his cap with the other to stop it blowing off in the wind.

'Right,' Jack said, as the sidecar was halfway down Grafton Street. 'Let's do it.'

Con pulled up alongside, Jack flicked off the safety catch on the pistol and levelled it at the officer's face. As he did so, McCormick turned to face him, removing his revolver from its holster in an effort to return fire. It was too late. Jack let off three shots. The first hit McCormick in the shoulder, the second and third hit him in the head. He slumped forward. The jarvey looked behind to see what had happened and saw the lifeless form of McCormick falling from the sidecar.

Jack hid the pistol under his jacket as Con drove the motorcycle in the direction of Trinity College. The street was full of Saturday shoppers carrying bags and dragging children as Con attempted to navigate his way through the crowds. But the jarvey had already cried out in terror seeing the blood-soaked body fall from his sidecar, alerting a nearby Civic Guard, who blew his whistle to attract the attention of his colleagues in the vicinity.

Con drove the motorcycle as fast as he could towards Trinity College, across College Green and onto Dame Street, where the bike's chain fell off, jamming the rear wheel and throwing the bike into a skid from which it was impossible to recover. Con tried to hang onto the bike but Jack was thrown clear as it skidded across the road and into the path of an oncoming tram. Jack was up on his feet and running in an instant. The tram had hit Con. There was blood everywhere. A crowd gathered around. Four Free State soldiers and a Civic Guard arrived at the scene. Con lay shaking, his left leg mangled by the tram wheels as Jack looked on helplessly.

'Run for it!' Con said, clenching his fists in an effort to quell the pain.

Jack stood there, not knowing what to do. It had all happened so quickly. First the shooting and then the crash.

A Guard came running from the direction of College Green shouting at the top of his voice.

'Stop that man! Stop that man!'

Jack turned to see the soldiers and bystanders looking at him. Reaching into his jacket he pulled out the Browning waved it in the air and began to run up Dame Street.

'Stop that man!' was all that he could hear.

His leg began to ache as he searched frantically for an escape route, hearing the whizzing sound of a bullet followed by the crack of a revolver from behind him. Stopping momentarily, he returned fire, sending the crowd of onlookers scurrying for cover as the four soldiers pointed their rifles at him. As one of the soldiers fell wounded and another went to his aid, Jack ran into Jury's Hotel in search of cover, two soldiers and two Civic Guards hot on his trail. Within minutes a Crossley tender filled with armed troops had arrived on the scene and Jury's was surrounded.

Jack ran up the stairs and kicked in the door of a room that overlooked Dame Street. Short of breath, he looked out the window. The pain in his leg grew. Feeling the sticky warmth of blood running down his face, he reasoned that he had been hurt when he fell off the bike. The blood continued to flow, some of it into the corner of his left eye, as he saw yet more troops arrive on the scene.

Searching his pockets for ammunition, Jack sat with his back against the window, facing the door. He had only three rounds left in his pistol.

The sound of troops entering the hotel and climbing the stairs filled his ears. There was no possible escape.

'To die or to surrender? That's what it's all come down to,' Jack said to himself, almost laughing as he pointed the pistol at the door.

'Come out of there. There's no escape. Throw down your weapon and come out. We won't shoot,' came the authoritative voice of a soldier.

'You'll have to come in and get me,' Jack replied, emptying his pistol at the door, in the hope that it might give him a little time to consider his options. There was no escape, only death.

'Drop your weapon and come out with your hands up or we'll shoot you.'

Jack sat back against the wall again feeling the blood pour from his head-wound.

'Is this what it has all been for? To die for Irish freedom? To make a better world? I'm sorry father, I'm sorry I've let you down,' he said, holding his head in his hands as the door was kicked in and several soldiers came through the doorway, revolvers in their hands.

'Drop your weapon or we'll shoot,' an officer said in a distinctly English accent.

Jack threw the Browning away from him in disgust. The

soldiers surrounded him and pulled him to his feet. The officer stood opposite him, raised his revolver, put the barrel in Jack's mouth and smiled.

'We've got you now, Paddy,' he said, as Jack noticed the Free State uniform on his obviously English captor.

One of the soldiers brought the stock of his rifle up sharply, hitting Jack's open head wound, sending him falling unconscious to the floor. It was over.

Jack awoke the following day in the hospital wing of Mountjoy Gaol. Through his blurred vision he could see several men in the ward, each of them bandaged in one way or another.

'Jack, are you still with us?' came a familiar voice.

'Terry? Is that you?' Jack asked, unable to see clearly.

'Aye, it's me. They got me a few weeks ago, filled me full of bullets, but they couldn't kill me,' he said bitterly.

Jack moved uneasily in his hospital bed, attempting to sit up.

'Are you okay?' Jack asked.

'I'm fine. I'll never play hurling again, but I'm fine. I heard what happened to you. It was bad luck, Jack. That's all—just bad luck,' Terry said.

'Have you heard anything about Con? Is he okay?'

'He's over in the other ward—they took his left leg off, poor fellah,' Terry said, shaking his head.

'Have you seen Jimmy at all?'

'He's over on one of the wings—A Wing, I think.'

'He's all right isn't he?'

'Jimmy's fine,' Terry replied. 'It's you I'm worried about.'

'We did what we had to do,' Jack said, feeling the dull pain in his head return.

***

Once his head-wound had closed and a doctor had examined him and considered him fit enough, Jack was transferred to A-Wing. Expecting to find Jimmy, he was told that he had been moved up to D-Wing a few days earlier.

Life on the wing was quiet and desperate. Everyone who was arrested after the amnesty had come to an end knew that they might face a firing squad if the special military courts deemed their offences serious enough.

'You can't get more serious than shooting an officer,' Jack said, sitting back on the bed in his cell as he discussed his fate with John O'Reilly, his cellmate.

O'Reilly agreed.

'Once you've been caught with a gun in your hand you don't stand a chance, Jack,' he said sympathetically.

'How were you caught?' Jack asked.

'It was on a raid against government administration offices. There were two units involved: one with some mines to damage the building, and the rest of us to keep the Staters and Guards back. The mining party was spotted as they tried to get into the building and a gunfight started with some Staters who turned up. Most of the lads got away, except Paddy Ryan and myself. We were cornered and they got us when we ran out of cartridges. I'm sure we were sold-out by an informer. There was no way out of it,' O'Reilly replied, staring at the cuts on his hands.

'When were you caught?' Jack asked.

'Two days after the amnesty ended. My trial is tomorrow.'

'Where are they taking you?'

'Beggar's Bush Barracks. That's where they're taking all the lads who were arrested after the amnesty. I'll be taken down there in the morning.'

'What do you think they'll do?'

'I think they'll shoot me,' O'Reilly said, resigned to his fate.

Jack shook his head as he felt a shiver run down his spine. He wondered, on seeing O'Reilly's blank expression, how the Staters could continue to execute their former comrades.

'Bastards,' Jack said, clenching his fists. 'I wish I was still on the run, I'd give the bastards something to think about.'

'It's over for me, Jack,' O'Reilly said. 'Don't bother yourself getting angry, there's nothing you can do about it anymore. The fight is over, we've lost.'

'But there are more men who'll take our place,' Jack said, thinking ahead.

'I wonder. They've executed around twenty volunteers since they started less than a month ago. No one likes those odds. Arms are being dumped all over the country; the war won't last much longer. The fight has left us,' O'Reilly said, looking at Jack.

There was a deep sadness in his eyes the likes of which Jack had never seen. They reminded him of Liam Mellows' eyes—full of knowledge and pain.

'Are you ready for it?' Jack asked, wondering if anyone could ever be ready for death.

'We're blessed in many ways, you and I, Jack. We have what very few people in this world have—a chance to say our goodbyes, a chance to repent for any wrongs we have done, to prepare for our end. Most people don't have that luxury,' he said with a smile. 'We've done all we could do and no one can take that away from us—even if they take our lives. What we have done will live forever in the hearts and minds of the Irish people. And no one will ever forget what the Staters have done. Forgive your enemy, Jack. Prepare yourself for the end.'

Jack closed his eyes and thought of his mother and how she must be feeling. Perhaps she didn't know how he had been caught, what he had done or what his fate might be.

He thought of Kathy and Helen and how they would suffer because of what he had chosen to do.

Jack sighed heavily, feeling the weight of sorrow pressing down on him. He knew how much he had hurt the ones he loved. None of it made sense anymore.

Jack's contemplation was broken by the sound of tin mugs being banged off the walls of the wing. There was a growing sense of unease, punctuated by the sounds of shouting. From the landing below the voice of a lone volunteer rose with the words of a newly written song. The wing fell silent, all ears listening to the words.

Take it down from the mast, Irish traitors,
The flag we Republicans claim.
It can never belong to Free Staters,
You've brought on it nothing but shame.

You've murdered brave Liam and Rory,
You've taken young Richard and Joe.
You hands with their blood are all gory,
Fulfilling the work of the foe.

But we stand with Enright and Larkin,
With Daly and Sullivan bold.
We'll break down the English connection,
And bring back the nation you sold.

So leave it to those who are willing,
To uphold in war or in peace:
The ones who intend to defend it,
Until England's tyranny cease.

The singing died away after a few minutes, leaving Jack alone with his thoughts until the screws called lights-out. It was quiet now on the wing.

Jack was woken early next morning by a screw banging on the door of the cell.

'O'Reilly, get your things together, it's your big day, today,' he laughed, as Jack's cellmate silently collected his belongings.

'Here, Jack, see if you can get my pocket watch to my mother, will you? I don't trust the Staters with it. Give it to one of the lads who was brought in before the amnesty—the address is written on a piece of paper inside,' O'Reilly said, handing Jack his watch.

'I'll be with you shortly, comrade,' Jack said, shaking O'Reilly's hand firmly. 'Be strong.'

'I will,' O'Reilly replied with a smile.

Two screws led him from the cell.

Jack sat down on his cot. His mind ran free. He remembered the night he and Terry had eaten dinner in his mother's house before the convention in City Hall, he remembered meeting Cathal Brugha in Mulligan's. He remembered seeing Liam Mellows when they entered the Four Courts and how happy he felt on seeing his old commander, how everything made sense back then. But the last few months had distorted the picture of his reality and it no longer bore any resemblance to what he had loved so dearly. Gone was the certainty, gone was the confidence. All that remained was the sorrow and pain. As he began drifting off to sleep a screw came to the door.

'Larkin, you're being transferred to the Bush Barracks in the morning,' he said with a smile. 'They'll sort you out over there in no time at all.'

'It'll be nice to get away,' Jack said calmly.

The screw's smile vanished beneath a look of disbelief.

'They're going to shoot you. You know that, don't you?' the screw asked.

'I know.'

'You're allowed to write a letter to your relatives. Here's a pencil and some paper,' the screw said coldly, leaving them on the bed.

Jack said nothing and looked down at the blank sheet of paper. Collecting his thoughts he sat back on the bed and began to write.

Jack was woken at six the following morning and taken to Beggar's Bush Barracks in a prison van. There he was brought before a special military court and tried for the killing of Officer Myles McCormick and the possession of a Browning LE automatic pistol.

Epilogue

December 13th 1923

Kathy stood silently in the rain outside Beggar's Bush Barracks on Haddington Road. She had been there since daybreak. Jack's sister and mother stood beside her. His mother held a set of rosary beads in her hands, slowly running her fingers over them as she prayed. Helen's eyes were red and swollen from crying.

A Free State soldier opened the gates at seven forty-five and handed a letter to each of the three families that were waiting to hear the fate of their loved ones.

Helen took the letter from the soldier, opened it, and read aloud:

'I am to inform you that Jack Larkin was tried under the Special Powers Act in a military court. He was found guilty of murder and was sentenced to death. This sentence will be executed on the morning of December 13th 1923 at eight o'clock.'

Jack's mother began to shake her head slowly on hearing Helen read the letter. Tears streamed down her face as she continued to pray. Helen quietly folded the letter. She began to shake uncontrollably.

Kathy stared blankly at a small spot on the barracks wall. The rain had begun to soak through her coat and she could feel the cold December air reaching into her bones. She imagined the cold wet earth where Jack would soon fall. It was almost eight o'clock. She could feel her heart beating faster and faster as every second passed; she could feel

Jack's presence.

As the bells of a nearby church marked the hour, Kathy's legs gave way. She slumped to the ground, feeling an unimaginable pain sweep through her body.

A volley of shots rang out.

Also published by Killynon House Books

Paddy Maguire is Dead

Lee Dunne

Available from May 2006

The novel *Paddy Maguire is Dead* by best-selling author Lee
Dunne was banned by the Irish Censors in 1972. Now for the
first time ever this controversial novel is available in Ireland -
thirty-four years after it was deemed indecent and obscene for
the Irish reading public.

Paddy Maguire is Dead is the continuation of Dunne's famous
novel *Goodbye to the Hill*, which has been described by critics
as a seminal novel of Dublin in the 1950s. *Paddy Maguire is
Dead* is a semi-autobiographical novel about a Dublin writer's
descent into alcoholism. It explores the harrowing effects
this killer disease can have on the family unit and how it can
destroy a man's career.

ISBN: 1-905706-02-2